Worth Fighting For

Also from Laura Kaye

Warrior Fight Club Series
FIGHTING FOR EVERYTHING
FIGHTING FOR WHAT'S HIS
FIGHTING THE FIRE (April 2019)

Blasphemy Series
HARD TO SERVE
BOUND TO SUBMIT
MASTERING HER SENSES
EYES ON YOU
THEIRS TO TAKE
ON HIS KNEES

Raven Riders Series
RIDE HARD
RIDE ROUGH
RIDE WILD
RIDE WILD
RIDE DIRTY

Hard Ink Series
HARD AS IT GETS
HARD AS YOU CAN
HARD TO HOLD ON TO
HARD TO COME BY
HARD TO BE GOOD
HARD TO LET GO
HARD EVER AFTER
HARD AS STEEL
HARD EVER AFTER
HARD TO SERVE

Hearts in Darkness Duet
HEARTS IN DARKNESS
LOVE IN THE LIGHT

Worth Fighting For

By Laura Kaye

A Warrior Fight Club/Big Sky Novella

Introduction by Kristen Proby

EVIL EYE
CONCEPTS

Worth Fighting For: A Warrior Fight Club/Big Sky Novella
By Laura Kaye
Copyright 2019
ISBN: 978-1-970077-09-4

Published by Evil Eye Concepts, Incorporated

An Introduction to the Kristen Proby Crossover Collection

Everyone knows there's nothing I love more than a happy ending. It's what I do for a living–I'm in LOVE with love. And what's better than love? More love, of course!

Just imagine, Louis Vuitton and Tiffany, collaborating on the world's most perfect handbag. Jimmy Choo and Louboutin, making shoes just for me. Not loving it enough? What if Hugh Grant in *Notting Hill* was the man to barge into Sandra Bullock's office in *The Proposal*? I think we can all agree that Julia Roberts' character would have had her hands full with Ryan Reynolds.

Now imagine what would happen if one of the characters from my Big Sky Series met up with other characters from some of your favorite authors' series. Well, wonder no more because The Kristen Proby Crossover Collection is here, and I could not be more excited!

Rachel Van Dyken, Laura Kaye, Sawyer Bennett, Monica Murphy, Samantha Young, and K.L. Grayson are all bringing their own beloved characters to play – and find their happy endings – in my world. Can you imagine all the love, laughter and shenanigans in store?

I hope you enjoy the journey between worlds!

Love,
Kristen Proby

The Kristen Proby Crossover Collection features a new novel by Kristen Proby and six by some of her favorite writers:

Kristen Proby – Soaring with Fallon
Sawyer Bennett – Wicked Force
KL Grayson – Crazy Imperfect Love
Laura Kaye – Worth Fighting For
Monica Murphy – Nothing Without You
Rachel Van Dyken – All Stars Fall
Samantha Young – Hold On

Acknowledgments from the Author

Writing this book has meant so much to me, not just because I so cherish writing stories about veterans and their families, which I do. But also because it was the first book I wrote after an unexpectedly serious surgery, so I often felt I was fighting for this love story right alongside my characters. Getting to the end was a triumph for all three of us!

No book is ever a solo project, so I need to thank Lea Nolan and Stephanie Dray for the writing sprints, feedback, and cheerleading that helped me finish the book. Thanks also to Christi Barth who was always there checking on me and encouraging me. Thanks also to KP Simmon for being a voice of wisdom in my head. And of course thanks to the awesome Liz Berry for giving me a chance to work in her creative orbit— she's an amazing force of nature and I'm glad to call her friend.

I also want to thank Kristen Proby for inviting me to be a part of this fantastic crossover project. I adored *Waiting for Willa* and couldn't wait for Jesse and his family to find their way back to each other.

Next, I want to thank all the readers—particular my Reader Girls & Guys and Heroes—for all the amazing support and encouragement, to me personally and for my books. You guys are the best evah! Finally, I thank each of you for taking my characters into your hearts so they can tell their stories again and again. ~ LK

Sign up for the 1001 Dark Nights Newsletter
and be entered to win a Tiffany Lock necklace.

There's a contest every quarter!

Go to www.1001DarkNights.com to subscribe.

As a bonus, all subscribers can download
FIVE FREE exclusive books!

Dedication

You're worth fighting for. Yes, you.

Chapter 1

Nothing chased away nightmares and anxiety like nachos. At least, that was what Tara Hunter hoped.

"Anything else?" Matt asked from behind the bar at Murphy's, her favorite place in the neighborhood.

"A rum and Coke," Tara said, taking off her coat and unwinding the scarf from her neck. She settled both on the stool next to her. It was eleven o'clock on a Sunday night, and the bar was as quiet as she'd hoped it would be.

Having placed the order, though, she was back to having nothing to distract her from the way her heart wouldn't settle and her breathing couldn't quite calm. She knew *exactly* why her central nervous system was freaking out—because tomorrow was her first day on a new diving team, and that meant getting back in the water again. But knowing didn't mean she could always control it. Having insight into all the ways her brain was messed up only got her so far.

So Tara forced a deep breath and counted backward from five.

Five things she could see. Her reflection in the mirror that was the centerpiece of the big, carved bar. Her long wavy hair pretty much looked like she'd rolled out of bed, because she had. Without any makeup, her face appeared pale in the dim light of the bar.

What else?

The rows of bottles glinting gold and white in the spotlights all along the bar. A couple tucked into the last booth, sitting on the same side and totally wrapped up in each other. Outside the front window, unusual late-winter flurries blew on the night wind.

Tara took another deep breath.

Four things she could hear. The alternative rock song playing on the juke box. Ice clinking in a glass. She peered around, her gaze following the sounds of the other diners. A man sitting in the closest booth was talking on his phone, *loudly*, one of those people who talked louder on cell phones as if he thought he needed to force his voice down the line. At the other end of the bar from where she sat, a customer thanked the bartender as he slid off his stool.

That time, her breath came deeper, slower, calmer.

Keep going.

Three things she could feel. Her nipples against her sweater, because her anxiety attack hadn't been able to abide taking the time to put on a bra before she'd bugged out of her place and gone for a walk in the late-February air.

Matt delivered her drink, and Tara took a long pull from it, mentally adding the fizz of the soda as the next thing she could feel. The smooth, cool glass in her hands—that was the third.

The muscles of her shoulders began to relax. It was working. Keep going.

Two things she could smell. The warm spice of the rum in her drink. The almost stale, malty tang of beer which seemed to be common to every establishment that served it.

Her heartrate was normal again.

Finish it. She took another drink of her rum and coke.

One thing she could taste. She'd already used the rum, so she crushed an ice cube between her teeth and concentrated on the clean, cold taste of the frozen pieces quickly melting in her mouth.

She heaved one last deep breath, and the ease of doing so proved for the millionth time that immersing herself in her environment had the power to calm.

The bell over the front door jingled and a gust of unusually bitter wind followed, enough to make Tara hug herself as she glanced over her shoulder to see who else was coming to Murphy's so late.

She almost choked on the ice cube in her mouth.

Because the man sliding onto a stool about five down from hers was freaking *gorgeous*. Tall. Broad shoulders with a trim waist, the quintessential swimmer's build she knew so well after a lifetime of being around swimmers and a career in diving. His black hair was cut short, and his face in profile was a study in hard angles—the square jaw, the high cheekbones, the furrowed brow. She hadn't seen him in Murphy's before. No way she would've forgotten—or missed—him.

Dark eyes slashed toward her.

When her heart kicked up in her chest this time, it had nothing to do with the nightmares she knew so well. And despite getting caught checking him out, Tara managed a smile. "Hey."

As he shrugged out of his coat, his gaze ran over her face, making her remember she hadn't done a *thing* to herself before walking out her door, and he nodded once. "Hey."

The bartender greeted New Guy and slid a coaster and a menu in front of him. "What'll you have?"

"Whiskey, neat, for now," the man said as he flipped open the menu.

Matt made the drink, then disappeared through the swinging doors into the kitchen. A minute later, he returned carrying a massive oval platter piled high with tortilla chips and toppings. He settled the plate in front of her.

"Holy shit, I forgot how big these were," she said with an incredulous laugh.

Matt grinned. "Maybe I'll steal one then."

"Steal two, Matt, seriously," she said, unrolling the napkin from around her silverware.

Her apartment was just down the block, and since she'd frequented Murphy's so much over the past year, she was on a first-name basis with most of the staff. He gave her a wink as he moved down to New Guy. "Care for anything else?"

The guy's gaze swung to Tara. "Are those as good as they look?" He had a slight drawl when he spoke, and Tara couldn't quite place it. It wasn't pronounced enough to be from someplace like Texas.

She smiled as she pulled a chip from the pile, the melted cheese stretching before it broke. "They're freaking awesome. There's just a metric crap ton of them."

He chuffed out a laugh. "So I see." He peered at the menu again, giving her a chance to appreciate the bulk of his biceps under a dark gray Henley. Because wow. "What else would you recommend that's not that big?"

Tara mmmed around the first chip. The crunch of it combined with the gooeyness of the cheese and sour cream and the tanginess of the pico and chili. Oh yeah, getting out of her apartment was exactly what she'd needed.

Matt tapped at the plastic-covered menu in front of the guy. "Wings are good. Pretzel sticks and cheese dip are real good. The loaded potato skins and onion rings are also great, though they're pretty big, too."

New Guy glanced at her nachos again.

"You could share mine. I'll never eat all these." Tara wasn't sure what possessed her to make the offer, except that there was no way she was going to finish them on her own.

The guy's eyebrow went up, and she couldn't tell if he was dubious or intrigued.

She shrugged as she ate a second chip. "Up to you, but if you don't decide soon I'll have eaten all the best ones."

Amusement played around his mouth. "There are best ones?"

"Of course there are best ones," she said, sucking sour cream off her finger.

The guy looked between her and Matt as if he was waiting for the punchline, and then his gaze latched onto hers. "What other appetizers do you like here?"

"Onion rings or wings, hands down."

Matt chuckled. "She's a regular."

"No kidding," New Guy said. "Let's go with the wings." The words were barely out of his mouth when he picked up his things and slid down to the bar stool right beside her. "You sure about this?" His shoulders were broad enough that they nearly touched. And he was even better looking up close. Laugh lines crinkled the corners of his eyes. Two character-adding scars jagged on his forehead. A hint of black ink curled up the side of his neck.

"I offered, didn't I?" She smirked.

He smirked back but held out a hand. "I'm Jesse. What's your name?"

The move seemed a little old-fashioned, but she found it charming nonetheless. She returned the shake, thinking that his name fit the accent. "Tara."

"Tara," he repeated, as if trying out her name to see how it felt on his tongue. She liked the way it sounded in his deep voice. Jesse grabbed a laden chip. "What makes a chip better or worse, Tara?" he asked as he took a bite.

"Well, obviously, the more toppings it has, the better it is. And the less toppings, the worse. And the crunchier chips are better than the ones that get soft under the cheese."

He hummed around a bite. "You have clearly put a lot of thought into this."

"Clearly. Or maybe I just know what I like," she said, instantly hearing the innuendo in the words. And his double-take revealed that he heard it, too. And *Holy Hot New Guy* why hadn't she brushed her hair or at least put on some tinted lip balm before coming out tonight?

"Good to know," he said with a chuckle. For a moment, they ate in silence, an odd intimacy between them from sharing the same plate of food. And then Jesse said, "So what's a girl like you doing at a place like this at midnight all by yourself?"

Tara laughed. Then realized that he hadn't been trying to make a joke. "Oh. *Oh.* You're serious." She laughed again. "Uh, what's a guy like you doing at a place like this at midnight all by yourself?"

His expression immediately read chagrinned. "Fair point. And I didn't mean for that to come out as quite that big of an idiot."

"That's good or you'd be relegated to the soggy chips."

"That's hardcore." He grinned at her. And, *man*, that grin. It managed to be both sexy and reserved, like he couldn't quite give in fully to the humor. And *that* impression was intriguing. Because she knew what it felt like to experience life as if through a filter. You on one side. The rest of the world on the other. And you could never quite get to where everyone else was. Maybe it was like that for everyone who'd died and come back to life.

Except, nope. She was cutting off *that* line of thinking right now. Or else she'd end up needing to count backward from five again.

He took a chip absolutely straining under a load of cheesy, gooey goodness, and Tara arched a skeptical brow that pulled a deep belly laugh from him. She loved the sound of that, too, which made the sarcastic retort she'd been thinking up get stuck in her throat.

Jesse shrugged with one big shoulder. "All I meant was what are the odds that I'd come in here and meet someone like you?"

Tara froze with a chip halfway between the plate and her mouth, and her heart kicked up in her chest. Was he teasing her now? Or flirting with her? Or both? "Someone like me?"

The smile he gave her was genuine. "Yeah, a pretty woman willing to share her nachos with a stranger."

Her mouth dropped open. Did he just call her pretty? "I don't even have any make-up on," she blurted.

His gaze ran over her face. "I didn't notice that."

Heat absolutely bloomed over her cheeks, and not a little licked down her spine, too. "Uh." She swallowed. "I couldn't sleep."

Now his glance was more appraising. "Me neither. Sometimes it helps me to walk when I can't sleep, which is what led me here."

"Me, too," Tara said, wondering what in the world was happening. Because it was *not* every day that she met a freaking gorgeous guy who not only complimented her but with whom she had things in common. "Of all the gin joints in all the towns in all the world, he walks into mine." She blinked, more heat filling her face as she realized she'd actually voiced the line that'd popped into her head. No one ever accused her of being smooth.

His grin was crooked. "I doubt they have 'As Time Goes By' on the jukebox."

Casablanca was her favorite movie. Beautifully, devastatingly romantic. "You know Casablanca?"

"Of course. One of the best movies of all time."

"Right? Wow. I think this is the beginning of a beautiful friendship." She raised her glass, more than a little embarrassed by her own cheesiness but having fun nonetheless.

Dark eyes intense, he clinked his tumbler against hers. They drank, eyes connected over the rims of their glasses. Butterflies whirled in Tara's belly, making her feel like she'd just crested the highest hill on a roller coaster.

Matt arrived with Jesse's wings. "Can I get y'all anything else?"

"Need a refill?" Jesse asked, nodding at her nearly empty glass.

"Yeah, sure," she said, even though a second was going to make her alarm going off painful come morning. Still, the sweet, fuzzy heat spreading through her blood felt good. And whether that was from the alcohol or her unexpected dinner companion, Tara wanted more of it.

Nodding, Jesse pushed the plate of wings between them. "Dig in."

Grinning, she grabbed a wing. "I love meals made out of just appetizers. You get a little bit of everything."

"So you like appetizers, late-night walks, *Casablanca*, and Murphy's, where you're a regular," Jesse said, taking a few wings for himself. "What else?"

She chuckled. "I don't know. I'm not that interesting."

He arched a brow, and it communicated disagreement so loud that she had to resist squirming on her stool.

"Um, I like swimming. And fighting." His expression went incredulous, and it made her grin and shake her head. "Not like, beating-people-up fighting. I belong to an MMA training club." She didn't offer more about it, because she really didn't want to get into the fact that Warrior Fight Club was for wounded warriors. Because too often she'd met guys who backed off when they found out she was a veteran. Worse, he might ask how she'd been wounded—something he'd be able to see for himself if he got a look at the other side or base of her throat. She was too much enjoying being fun, flirty Tara. For tonight, she didn't want to be almost-died Tara.

Jesse scratched his jaw. "How you think that makes you not interesting, I have no idea."

She nodded to Matt when he brought her fresh drink, then took a long sip. The rum was sweet and smooth on her tongue. "How about you? Tell me some random things you like."

He shrugged and his eyes narrowed as he thought about it. "The Pacific Ocean. The way the mountains come right up to the beach in California."

"Is that where you're from?"

He gave a head shake as he ate another nacho. "I've lived there on and off over the past decade, but I'm originally from Cunningham Falls, Montana."

That explained the accent, and it gave her pictures of him on horseback, a cowboy hat on his head. And she did not mind those images one bit. "I've never been."

His gaze went distant. "I haven't been back in a long time."

"Still have family there?" she asked, immediately regretting the question when his jaw went tight, making her feel like she'd veered into territory he didn't want to cover.

"Yeah."

The shortness of his answer made it clear she'd read him right, so Tara changed the topic. "What brought you to DC?"

"A new job." He took a drink of his whiskey, then stared for a long moment at their reflection in the bar's mirror. "How 'bout you? DC home for you?"

The water was always where she'd felt most at home. Right up until a broken cable had sliced through the ocean and nearly garroted her. Other than that, she wasn't sure. Her dad had been in the navy, so they'd moved around a lot when she'd been a kid, and then her own naval career had meant more of the same. "It has been for the past year. Before that, a little bit of everywhere."

Jesse slanted her a grin. "Citizen of the world, then?"

Omigod, she was never going to survive this sexy man quoting Casablanca to her. Never. A ripple of delighted excitement ran through her belly. "Yeah. Exactly."

He gave her a crooked grin and winked. *Freaking winked!* If Tara hadn't been sitting on that bar stool, her panties might've dropped to her ankles.

"I hear that," he said as he raised his glass to her. "To putting down new roots."

"Um, I'll drink to that," she managed as they clinked. "So what else do you like?"

"Let's see," he continued. "I like anything to do with the water. Swimming, boating, surfing, scuba." So she'd been right about that swimmer's physique then. "I used to do a lot of skiing, too. There was great skiing near where I grew up." Something dark and distant passed over his expression. For just a moment, she was sure of it. But then it was gone as fast as it'd appeared. "Haven't done much of it in years now, though."

She wasn't touching the Montana topic again, so she sipped her rum and Coke and just enjoyed the unexpected companionship. On the juke box, the song changed, and Tara grinned. "Oh, my God. I danced to this at prom," she said as an old Journey power ballad played.

He smirked at her. "What was the guy's name?"

Tara snorted. "Curtis Miles. We were just friends. Or so I thought, until he started crooning 'When You Love a Woman' in my ear as we danced. Except he changed the *you* to *I*. It was super awkward."

Jesse chuckled. "Poor guy."

"Don't feel bad for him. He ended up hooking up with one of my friends later that night."

"Damn. Sorry."

Tara shook her head. "No need. I didn't mind and the two of them have been married for twelve years and have three kids. They were clearly meant to be."

"You believe in that?" He signaled to Matt for a refill of whiskey.

"What?"

Jesse slanted her a look. "Meant to be."

Twisting her lips, Tara shrugged. "It sure seems to be true for some people." She thought of her coupled WFC friends. Noah and Kristina had been best friends since childhood and were now together. That sure seemed meant to be. And Billy and Shayna had also known one another since she was a teenager and had been roommates before dating, so that seemed like it might've been meant to be, too.

Jesse's expression grew thoughtful as he reached for his fresh drink. "Maybe for some people it is."

A weighted silence settled between them. It wasn't uncomfortable, exactly, but the exchange had definitely held up in front of her eyes that there didn't seem to be a *meant to be* for her. Or else she wouldn't be nearly thirty-two with only one long-term relationship under her belt—one that hadn't survived her injuries and medical discharge from the navy.

Tara mentally pushed the thoughts away as she wiped her mouth and dropped the napkin on her plate. "The more important question is, do you like dessert?"

He laughed, and the deep rumble of it made her smile. "I've been known to enjoy dessert now and again."

Was it just her or did that sound like he was talking about something besides a sugary treat at the end of a meal? "Have you now?"

He turned on his stool toward her, and his knee pressed against her thigh. "Just what is it you're tempting me to share with you now?"

Heat slinked through her blood, the arousing sensation originating from where they touched. "The monster ice cream sundae," she said, hoping he didn't pick up on the breathiness suddenly coloring her voice.

One side of his mouth quirked up. "Define monster."

"Three scoops of chocolate and vanilla ice cream. Chocolate and caramel sauces. Chocolate chips, whipped cream, and a cherry. All on top of a warm chocolate chip cookie. I can never order it by myself because it's too big so you'd be doing me a huge favor."

His arched an eyebrow, his expression seriously sexy. "Is that right?"

"Mmhmm."

A crooked smile broke through his smirk. "Okay, then. Sounds great. Consider me tempted, Tara." The flirtation in his words was mirrored by the amusement playing around his mouth and an intriguing intensity in his eyes.

She turned toward where Matt stood wiping down menus. "Give us the sundae, please?"

"You got it," the bartender said.

Tara looked back to Jesse. "I hope you think it's as great as it sounds."

His gaze ran over her face again, a slow, purposeful perusal that trailed heat low into her belly. "I'm sure it will be. This has already been one of my best meals in a long damn time."

"Murphy's is fantastic, isn't it?"

He nodded. "From what I've tried so far, it seems like it is. But I was talking more about the company than the food."

The directness of his words nearly stole her breath. "Wow. I, uh, I have to agree," she managed, smiling even as her head spun with the chemistry zinging between them. She had no idea where it might lead, but the longer they hung out, the more she hoped this meal wouldn't be the last she saw of this man.

Chapter 2

Jesse Anderson wasn't sure what the hell he was doing, but he was having fun doing it, and that was better than most of how he'd felt lately. So he was rolling with it.

After sharing appetizers with Tara, they'd polished off their sundae, too. "I'm really glad you didn't say it was too cold for ice cream," she said, a soft waterfall of brown waves framing her pretty face as she peered over at him. "I don't think we could've stayed friends if you had."

"That would've been a damn shame." He smirked teasingly, thoroughly enjoying their banter, her sense of humor, and the unusual feeling of possibility he felt just being in her presence. When had he last enjoyed someone's company so much? He couldn't pinpoint it. Not surprising given he'd spent so much of the last year since he'd left the navy alone. But it all just made him want more of how she was making him feel. "Besides, nobody needs that kind of negativity in their life," he said, loving the sound of her ready laughter. She was just easy to talk to and be with.

"Right? I completely agree." Her blue eyes danced with amusement.

The bartender gestured to the now-empty dish. "All done here?" When they agreed, he asked, "How do you want to do the check?"

"I'll get it," Jesse said.

"Give it to me," Tara said at the same time.

They looked at each other and laughed.

"You have to let me get it." She arched a brow at him. "The nachos were mine anyway. And I talked you into the sundae."

Jesse squashed the reflex born of his upbringing to debate it and grasped onto a potential opportunity instead. "My treat next time then?"

Her eyebrows lifted as if he'd surprised her, and then the sexiest smile brightened her face. "Deal."

A warm satisfaction filled his gut, and Jesse held up his hands. "Give it to the lady." Matt nodded, took Tara's card, and moved down to the computer terminal. And then Jesse made something crystal clear. "But for the record, you didn't really need to talk me into anything. I was willing all the way."

Pink bloomed over her cheeks, and Jesse found himself enjoying all the different reactions he'd managed to pull out of her over the course of their meal. "Good to know," she said, tucking a long wave of hair behind her ear. "Excuse me for a minute. Restroom."

He nodded and watched her head deeper into the now emptier bar. The knee-high brown boots over a pair of form-fitting jeans that did all kinds of justice to her curves were a killer combination. Not to mention the sway of all those soft waves that tumbled nearly to her waist. Damn, this woman appealed to him on so many levels. Which made him wonder when that *next time* might be.

It made him hopeful that DC was going to provide the clean slate he really needed it to be. New place, new job, new...friend. New chance to build a life and a career where he didn't let people down. All the fucking time.

His cell buzzed in his pocket, and he retrieved it to find a text from his mom. *Hi Jesse – just wanted to let you know I shared your new number with Willa and everyone so don't be surprised if you get some calls or messages. Let me know how your first day goes tomorrow. Love you, Mom*

Disparate reactions flooded through him. The comfort of being in touch with his mother. The discomfort of just how distant his relationships with his mother and sister were—his fault, of course. And just one more way he'd messed up.

Footsteps from his right alerted him to Tara's return, and he looked up from checking his phone to see her coming his way. With curves for days and a soft, sexy smile just for him.

That was when he noticed it. A deep slash of a scar that ran diagonally down the right side of her throat. Jesus, he couldn't begin to imagine what had caused something that pronounced. He'd seen enough injuries to know she'd survived something major—and she'd tried to say she wasn't interesting.

"Hey," he said.

She gave his face an appraising glance, one that told him she'd noticed what had caught his attention. "Hey. Oh, let me not forget this." She pocketed her credit card and signed the receipt.

Then they were sliding on coats and making for the door.

Outside, the air was crisply cold, and he relished the invigorating feeling of it in his lungs. A thin layer of snow crunched underfoot. An occasional car passed by, but mostly it was quiet, peaceful. Tara turned toward him, and all Jesse knew was that, despite needing to be up at oh dark hundred tomorrow for his new job, he wasn't ready to go back to his hotel. And, truth be told, he wasn't ready to part from her either.

She smiled. "So…"

"Any chance you feel like walking for a while?" he asked, just as the wind gusted, swirling the long ends of her hair around her shoulders. "I get it if it's too late or too cold."

Glancing down, she crushed a ball of snow under her boot. Jesse was sure she was going to turn him down. "No, actually, I'd like that. Walk off some of those nachos."

"And the wings."

"And the ice cream."

He grinned. "Have a preferred direction?"

She pointed to the left down M Street. "That way takes us past the Naval Yard, or"—she pointed toward the right—"that way would take us down to the waterfront and The Wharf."

The last thing he wanted to do tonight was to think about the navy. He'd retired the day he'd gotten his twenty, so it'd been his choice to get out. His choice, also, to parlay a lifetime devoted to combat diving and EOD into a new career in commercial diving. Except there was a little voice in his head that said he'd had no choice at all—not when he'd failed to bring home all his techs. Not when he'd lost eight during the twenty-six-month period before he'd called it quits.

He had to clear the emotion from his throat. "How about to the waterfront?"

"Waterfront it is."

"You lead and I'll follow," he said, enjoying the small smile she gave him. And that she'd agreed to the walk. It made him wonder why she hadn't been able to sleep, and whether she hadn't wanted to go home either. It was strange in a good way to think she might understand how he felt.

Then again, he could be overthinking the whole thing.

They walked side by side down the wide sidewalk, passing mostly dark restaurants and coffee shops, or bars closing up just like Murphy's had been. For more than a block, they didn't talk, but Jesse didn't think the quiet felt awkward.

"How long have you been in DC?" she finally asked.

"Not quite a week."

Her eyes went wide. "So do you have an apartment yet?"

He shook his head. "No, I'm in a Courtyard Marriott for a few weeks until I find a place to stay."

"Oh, the one by Murphy's?" she asked, and he nodded. "I think you're like a block away from me then."

That was good to know. "Yeah?"

"I'm in the red-brick apartment building with the coffee shop, bagel place, and pizzeria down at street level."

"That's like everything you need in your whole life all in one place."

Her whole face lit up as she laughed. "Right? It's expensive as hell but those helped sell me. What part of the city are you looking at?"

"I'd like to stay by the water if I can find something I like, but I've just started looking."

She enumerated the pros and cons of several different nearby neighborhoods, some of which he'd started exploring for himself, and then made an offer that surprised him—in a good way. "If I can help, just let me know."

How had he gotten so lucky tonight to walk into that bar and meet someone as cool as Tara? And to maybe have the chance to see her again? Because good surprises were not the norm for him. Never had been. "You might regret making that offer," he teased.

"I doubt it, but if so, I think I can handle myself," she said with a sexy smirk.

Somehow, he didn't doubt it one bit. "Right, the MMA training."

"Mmhmm. For starters."

"Consider me intrigued."

She chuckled as they approached the intersection where they could cross over to the waterfront. "I probably shouldn't ruin my mystique by admitting that intriguing isn't how most people would describe me."

He threw her a skeptical look. To him, she was definitely fucking intriguing. Sexy and confident, outgoing and generous. "And how is it you think people would describe you?"

The *walk* sign flashed, and they started across the broad avenue. "I'm kind of a nerd."

Jesse barked out a laugh. "If you're a nerd—"

A blaring horn sounded out from their left. Jesse turned to find a cabby tearing through the intersection despite the red light. The yellow car swerved widely around them as Jesse grasped Tara by the shoulders and hauled her onto the median.

"Jesus," she gasped out, trembling underneath his hands.

"I'm sorry. I didn't mean to manhandle you," he said, realizing that he'd overreacted. But too many people had died on his watch, and he'd had to write too many letters to his guys' families, and the fucking reminder of all of that surged anger and adrenaline through his blood.

Wide blue eyes peered up at him. "God, don't apologize, Jesse. That guy was an asshole."

He wasn't sure why he found that funny, except that the letdown in the form of humor was probably better than the letdown he'd get from beating the shit out of something. "Yeah, he really fucking was," he said, giving her a wink.

She chuckled. "Welcome to DC."

He guffawed. "You really know how to show a guy a good time."

She gaped. Then smirked. Then punched him in the chest. "That wasn't my freaking fault." The words didn't hold any heat. He grasped the hand she'd smacked him with, and she stumbled into him, making them both chuckle.

Jesse peered down at her. He had a good seven or eight inches on her and, standing so close, she had to tilt her head way back to meet his gaze. Slowly the adrenaline and the humor and the whole damn night closed in around them, making him hyperaware of all the places her body touched his.

Hunger absolutely *tore* through his blood. His gaze dropped to the full bow of her lips. He wanted a taste of her so damn bad, but he didn't want to push her somewhere she didn't want to go.

Her fingers tightened around his, and their gazes collided. And thank *fuck*, he wasn't in this alone. Because he saw his own desire reflected back at him. In spades.

"Tara—"

"Yes," she said.

It was all the encouragement he needed.

His free hand slid into her hair and cupped the back of her head, pulling them together. And then his mouth was on hers. Just a press of skin to skin, but enough to chase the cold away. Especially when she fisted her hand in his coat and pulled herself closer.

"Damn," he gasped, winding his other arm around her back and hauling her in tight.

When his lips found hers again, they were parted, and the invitation was too hot to resist. His tongue swept into her mouth, tasting a hint of the sweetness of their dessert and something that was all Tara. And then her tongue stroked him in return, such a small thing for how fast it made him hard. And he wasn't the only one feeling the heat between them if the moan she unleashed was any indication, and it only made him want her more.

Jesus, where was this going? Jesse knew what he wanted—and it was Tara in his bed. Under him. On top of him. Taking him deep inside.

The strength of his desire for her made him pull back because they'd known each other for all of a few hours. Then they stood forehead to forehead, their panting breaths chasing the chill away.

"Hey," she said.

"Hey."

"It's not cold anymore." A seriously seductive humor played in those bright blue eyes.

"No, it's hot as hell."

She licked her lips, and the thought that she was tasting him there had him swallowing hard. "Should we walk more, or…"

"Sure," he said, really damn glad that she didn't seem scared off by whatever was happening between them. He stepped back and took her by the hand. He wasn't sure why he did it, except it felt like the most natural thing in the world. "This okay?"

"More than okay," she said, smiling up at him.

Along the river, the wind was stronger, more biting. They passed a marina where sailboats bobbed in the choppy water. The lights of the Wharf—a district of waterfront shops and restaurants he'd explored a few days before—sparkled another half mile in the distance. He was completely comfortable walking with her, but every once in a while, her hand trembled in his. "Why don't we cut back into the city? It'll be less windy."

"Sounds good."

They crossed over to I Street, heading back in the direction from which they'd come. "How cold are you?"

"Somewhere just south of human popsicle," she said, the tip of her nose a little red.

He chuckled. "We could catch a cab back," he said, knowing they had eight or ten of the city's wider blocks to get back to where they started.

"That's a thought," she said. "Or, um…"

He peered down at her. "What?"

Tara's cheeks went pink, and he didn't think it was just the weather. "Or, you know, you could kiss me again."

Need lanced through him. Jesse pulled her into the well of a doorway that provided a bit of a shield against the wind, and then his hands were in her hair and his mouth was on hers for several long, hot seconds. "Like that?" he rasped.

"Yes," she whispered.

"Maybe again, just to make sure you're warm enough." It only took her smiling for him to dip his mouth to hers once more. Her hands settled on his hips, making him hotter, but it was her sucking on his tongue that had him boxing her in against a wall. "Jesus."

She peered up at him, beautiful and brazen. "Definitely warmer now."

"Good. That's good," he said, taking her by the hand again and just barely resisting adjusting himself.

They made it another block and a half before he was the one initiating the kiss. He tugged her against the corner of a building. "Now I'm cold," he said, arching a challenging brow.

Her laughter lit him up inside. "Better bring those lips down here then."

He claimed her on a needful groan, the whole night suddenly feeling like extended foreplay. Not that he was complaining. Because he hadn't felt this good, this excited, this fucking *alive* in longer than he could say. He dragged his lips from her mouth and kissed her jaw, her ear, and the top of her throat not covered by the scarf.

"Better?"

"Much," he said.

They made it one more block before they found themselves in a temporary covered sidewalk along a construction site, and Tara stopped abruptly. Jesse gave her a questioning look, and found her tugging off her scarf. "My, um, now my neck is *really* cold."

Banked lust from their last kiss surged through him. He leaned back against one of the metal supports and tugged her to stand between his legs. "What would help that?"

"Maybe if you kissed me here," she said, touching the side of her throat without the scar.

God, her playfulness and willingness to ask for what she wanted were a seductive fucking combination. "I'll kiss you anywhere you want, Tara," he said, leaning down until he was kissing her neck, and all the while cataloguing the other body parts he'd like to get his mouth on next. And when he couldn't access as much of her skin as he wanted, he unzipped the top of her coat so that he could get to the tendon that ran outward to her shoulder.

Her hand scrabbled for purchase in his short hair. "God, Jesse."

His name in that aroused tone made him feel like she'd taken a blowtorch to his blood. He kissed and sucked and nipped until he was half certain they were going to end up having sex standing right there. "Christ, come on," he said, kissing her once again on the mouth before leading her through the covered sidewalk and out the other side.

After that, they barely made it a block at a time without getting their mouths and hands on one another until, finally, they found themselves across the street from his hotel.

"That's me," Jesse said, peering down at Tara and hoping he wasn't the only one strung absolutely tight from their mile-long make-out session.

"I'm about a block that way," she said, her breath frosting on the air.

"I could walk you to your door," he said, blood pounding in his veins. "Or you could come up. I know what I want, Tara, but it's your choice. Just say the word."

Chapter 3

"I'll come up," Tara said, taking a chance even as the city spun around her. Because things like this just didn't happen to her. At least, they never had before. And that seemed like a really good reason to hold tight to it and see where it was going.

Pure, raw satisfaction rolled over Jesse's expression, making her belly flip. Dark eyes blazed down at her. "You sure?"

Was she sure that she understood how something so awesome was happening? No, not at all. Was she sure she wanted whatever was coming next? Oh yeah. "I'm sure."

He squeezed her hand as they crossed the street. The very first time he'd grasped her palm, she'd nearly melted at how warm and unexpected and sweet it was. She'd still been doing a mental Snoopy dance over how amazing their kiss had been when he'd started dragging his thumb back and forth across her knuckles. And that had made her need the feel and the taste of him again.

Thank God he'd gone along with her solution for being cold. She adored that he seemed to enjoy her particular brand of probably goofy flirtation. Once, she would've been far too shy to suggest to a man that he kiss her, but then she'd nearly died, and ever since all the game-playing and beating-around-the-bush of life felt too much like wasting time she didn't really know she had.

Inside the lobby, both of them nearly groaned as the heat enveloped them. "God, that feels good," she said.

"Hell yes, it does," he said, taking them to the bank of elevators.

The doors to one eased open before them, and Tara stepped in, her belly doing another loop-the-loop at what was about to happen between them. Jesse hit the button for the seventh floor and then walked her backward until he'd trapped her in the corner. "Bet I can make you feel even better."

Heat pooled low in her belly. God, she wanted him. She didn't want to overthink it or debate it or question the right and wrong or smart and dumb of it, she just wanted this man. "I'm counting on it."

"Christ, Tara," he bit out. "Whatever you want or don't want, you gotta tell me now. Because once we get in my room, it's gonna be really fucking hard for me to not be all over you."

She squeezed her thighs together at the promise of his words, but it didn't give her the relief she needed—the relief she needed from *him*. "Jesse, I wouldn't be in this elevator with you if I didn't want you all over me." God, he was looking at her like he wanted to devour her, and she was so down with that.

The bell dinged their arrival to his floor, and the doors slid open.

"Thank God," he said, drawing her into the hallway with a speed and an urgency that was as hot as it was humorous, because she felt the same way. His room was the last one on the left. A quick swipe of his card had them nearly falling inside, hands and mouths all over each other, pulling off coats and shirts and shoes. "I want to see you," he said, flicking on a switch that illuminated the lamp next to the couch.

"Agreed." She shed her sweater to the floor where it joined both of their coats and his Henley, leaving both of them bare from the waist up and baring her second scar—the one at the base of her throat from the emergency tracheotomy she'd needed.

But she was too focused on how freaking hot he was to worry about her scars. Jesse had a tattoo that extended from the base of his throat, over his shoulder, and down his left arm—black stars connected by blue and gray swirls. And wow was his upper body a thing of muscled beauty. Lean and defined, with a thin covering of dark chest hair that trailed intriguingly beneath his jeans. There were scars, too, more than a few. The longer hair on top of his head was a finger-raked mess, and it was sexy as hell.

Given the number of times his hands had been in her hair tonight, she guessed she looked the same. "I don't want to miss any of this, otherwise I might convince myself that it was all a dream."

His grin was deliciously predatory as he closed the little distance between them, bringing them chest to chest. "Fuck, I'm torn between hot and fast or spreading you out and taking my damn time."

Yes, please. A shiver raced over her skin, because she wanted whatever he wanted. "Do we have to choose?"

"Jesus, maybe this is a dream," he said, hands undoing her jeans and roughly working them down over the flare of her hips. The frenzy of need picked up between them again, with her undoing his fly, revealing a pair of black cotton boxers pulled tight over the outline of his hard cock.

The air on her now heated skin unleashed another shiver. She ached between her legs from how long they'd teased each other and from the maddening anticipation of having him inside her. It'd been almost two years since she'd last had sex, and she was quite possibly *dying* for it.

Jesse retrieved a condom from his wallet as she pushed down his jeans and boxers until they hung around his knees.

"Oh, God, you're big," she breathed, taking him in hand and relishing the fascinatingly hard heat of him. She wanted him inside her more than anything she'd wanted in a long, long time.

When she gave him a tight stroke, he sucked in a harsh breath as he dropped his wallet to the floor and tore open the packet with his teeth. And that reaction was fascinating, too, seeing him so on edge because of her. "Christ, I need you."

He rolled the latex down his length, and then brought his fingers to her slit and slid them into the wetness hidden there. Tara moaned and her head snapped back against the wall.

"Fuck, you're so ready. Are you sure, Tara?"

"If you stop now I might literally die," she rasped, completely overwhelmed by her own desire.

He spun her to face the wall then grasped her hip with one hand while he guided his dick with the other. Then his head was at her opening and sinking home.

They both groaned as he worked himself into her until she'd taken him all, and then he gave her hot and fast, just like he'd promised.

Moans and curses and pleas spilled out of her lips. Because the feel of him was a freaking riot of sensation. The amazing, demanding fullness of his invasion. The impact of his hips against her ass. The tightness of his hold, with one hand gripping her hip and the other anchored around her shoulder.

And then he reached around with the hand that had been on her hip and slipped his fingers into the slick needy heat between her thighs. She nearly shouted at the goodness of it.

"Please make me come," she begged, nearly crying in relief when he hunched himself more tightly around her, the strokes of his cock shifting to more of a grind so that he could focus his attention on what his hand was doing. Rubbing her clit with quick, wet circles, then pushing between her lips so that the length of his long fingers stroked her so damn good.

"Already so fucking tight, Tara. You gonna squeeze me even harder?" The words were hot and harsh in her ear. Guttural. Perfect.

"Yes," she whined. "Please."

"Fuck, you're going to take me with you."

His words were joining with his fingers and his cock to shove her closer and closer to the edge. "Oh God."

The grinding turned into rough, amazing, punctuated thrusts. "Give it to me," he said, his voice absolutely raw.

She braced harder against the wall, shoving herself back on him as he hammered forward. And then he slapped her clit in time with one of those hard thrusts.

Tara's whole body detonated. She just flew apart into a million screaming pieces. The orgasm wracked through her in concentric circles that started where they were joined and left no part of her untouched. She couldn't think, couldn't speak, couldn't breathe. She was less standing than being held up by Jesse's sheer strength and possessive grip.

She'd never, *ever* felt anything so all-encompassing, so *shattering* in her whole life.

"Christ, I'm coming," Jesse groaned as his dick jerked inside her, hands tight on both of her hips, his whole body shuddering when his weight fell against her back.

Harsh panting breaths were the only sounds in the room.

Jesse exhaled heavily, and the rush of it ghosted across her neck. His hand went to where he was softening inside her, and Tara was already regretting what she knew was going to be the torturous emptiness that his withdrawal was going to leave behind.

"Let me get rid of this," he whispered, pressing a kiss against the scarred side of her throat.

"If you let go of me, I'm going to fall," she said, half teasing but also pretty sure it was true.

"Fuck if my motor skills are much better right now," he said, humor plain in his voice. He did withdraw then, though he kept one hand around her waist. "You okay?"

Still leaning against the wall, Tara smiled despite the shocking emptiness. "You mean except for the fact that you made my bones melt?"

He turned her, making her realize that her jeans still hung around her thighs—and so did his. "Please, go on."

Chuckling, Tara smacked the back of her hand against the deliciously hard plane of his abs. "Shut up."

Grinning, he kissed her. The sexy jerk. Then he tugged up his Levi's and crossed the room, giving her a chance to really admire the way all that ink moved over his shoulder and arm before he disappeared into what she guessed was the bathroom.

Tara fixed her own jeans and hugged her sweater to her chest as she wandered deeper into the suite. A small kitchenette and sitting room occupied the space right next to the door, with the bed taking up the far side of the room. In the wake of the mind-numbingly good sex, her thinking brain was starting to come back online now, which made her wonder what was next. If anything. They'd teased about that only being the first round, but that was when lust had hijacked both of their bodies.

"There are some drinks in the fridge. Help yourself," Jesse called out from the other room.

"Thanks," she said, pulling the sweater back over her head. She grabbed a bottle of water from the fridge and took a long sip.

Strong arms wrapped around her waist from behind, and Jesse settled his chin on her head. Surprise at the affectionate embrace whipped through her belly, which was maybe silly given everything else they'd shared tonight. "Hey," he said.

"Hey." She held her water bottle up to him. Why did it feel intimate when he accepted? A gut check told her why—because she didn't have this with anyone else in her life. She had friends, sure. Guy friends, too. But this kind of quiet intimacy? Or the intense physical intimacy from minutes before? No. Not in a long time. Hell, maybe never.

And since she'd only been in DC for the last year, none of those friends had yet become the kinds of BFFs with whom you shared absolutely everything.

So this felt different. Special. Kinda scary, but that was the thing about nearly dying—it made you willing to try, to reach, to take a chance. Well, at least outside of her work. Given what it'd taken her to get back in the water, that was one place where she played things safe. But this wasn't that.

When he gave her the nearly empty bottle, she turned in his arms, needing to see the cast of his eyes and the expression on his face. She didn't know Jesse well enough to read his quiet, so she needed these other cues. There was still an intensity in the way his dark gaze took her in, but his expression was all sated ease. She didn't think she was overstaying her welcome, but what was the point in wondering? "So, should I…go?"

He frowned. "Only if you want to, but I'm perfectly happy with you right where you are."

Smiling, Tara nodded. "Okay."

"There's something I'm not happy about though."

"Uh, and that is?" She finished the last of the water.

"You put your shirt on."

Tara smirked. "I figured if it was going to get awkward, it would be better if I was prepared to make a fast exit."

Jesse arched a brow. "Did it get awkward?"

She chuckled. "Not yet."

He slipped the bottle from her hand and tossed it into the recycling can, and the next thing she knew he'd bent and put her over his shoulder.

Tara burst out in an incredulous laugh, her hands grasping the hard, flexing muscles down his sides. "What are you doing?"

"Making it clear I want you to stay." He tossed her on the bed, making her laugh again as she bounced on the mattress and he climbed in until he was on hands and knees above her.

Whose life was she even living right now? A hot man had flirted with her, called her pretty, expressed interest in spending time with her, kissed her, fucked her senseless, *and* wanted to make sure she knew he was in no hurry for her to go. "Now I'm peeved," she said, forcing her lips into a playful pout.

His eyes narrowed. "Why's that?"

Having him above her was *all kinds* of distracting. And hot. How could she be hot again after the orgasm he'd just wrung out of her? "Because I didn't have time to grab your butt before you threw me on the bed."

Snickering, he grabbed her hand and put it on his ass. "That's a problem I can solve."

Grinning, Tara squeezed. "Mmm. Very nice."

He chuckled. "Literally grab any part of me you want. Consider it a standing invitation."

"I'll remember that."

Jesse lowered his weight on top of her, his big body settling into the cradle of her thighs, and *geez* it felt good. And then his expression went more serious. "I don't know what's happening here, Tara. I just know I like it."

"I feel all of that, too," she said, glad she wasn't in this...whatever it was...alone. And man did she appreciate him saying what he felt. If she had to guess, he was a few years older than her almost thirty-two. So maybe he'd reached a point in his life where he didn't see the sense in beating around the bush, either. Whatever explained his forthrightness, she liked it.

He lowered his face to hers and kissed her. Once, twice. Slow and lingering. Taking his time. Which made her remember what he'd said earlier.

"Fuck, I'm torn between hot and fast or spreading you out and taking my damn time."

A thrill whipped through her belly.

This time when he kissed her, his tongue swept into her mouth, exploring her, stroking her, tasting her. His hands went to her hair, but it was pinned under her back. "Hold on," she said, chuckling as she tugged the long length of it out and twisted it so it lay in a soft rope to her side. Belatedly, she realized that she'd pulled it to the unmarred side of her throat, leaving him a clear, close view of both of her scars.

She thought he was going to ask what'd happened, but then his gaze lifted to hers. And there was something there, some emotion that she didn't know him well enough to name. "Jesus, what if I'd never walked into Murphy's?"

The soft exclamation reached inside her chest and played with things that hadn't been played with in so, so long. "What if you'd thought I was crazy when I'd offered to share my nachos?"

He nodded. "What if you hadn't agreed to take a walk with me?"

"It would've been a tragedy," she said, injecting humor into the affection wrapping around her. Because affection for a man wasn't something she was used to feeling. Not in a long time.

He tugged at the side of her sweater. "You covered up again is a tragedy."

That had her grinning again. She arched her back and worked it over her head with his help. "There. That's a problem *I* can solve."

"Much better," he said, dipping his head to kiss and lick one of her nipples. Against her thigh, his erection grew.

Tara arched into his mouth and surrendered to him exploring her. "Is this Option B?"

He lifted his gaze to look up her body, and if she'd thought him gorgeous before, it was nothing to seeing him with arousal darkening his gaze and highlighting the harsh angles of his face. "Option B?"

Her hand went to his face, her fingers tracing his high cheek bone. Jesse turned his mouth into her touch, surprising her by licking her fingers and sucking two into his mouth. She gasped. "Yeah, um, spreading me out and taking your time."

The dark brown of his gaze absolutely blazed. "This is exactly fucking that." He flicked at her nipple with his tongue. "Any objections?"

The way he kept checking in with her made it even easier to agree. Tara shook her head, silent this time because she really had no words for what he was doing to her, for how he was overwhelming her. In all the best ways.

"Good. Get comfortable. Because I'm going to be a while."

Chapter 4

Jesse moved down Tara's body, intent on finally being able to put his mouth on her everywhere he'd been wanting. So after he took off her jeans and panties for the second time tonight, he got himself good and comfortable between her legs, forcing her with his shoulders to open wider. Then he kissed her thigh. And again. Then higher. Until he was licking her clit and sucking it into his mouth.

Tara's hands fisted in the comforter. The moan that spilled out of her went directly to his dick and had him licking her harder, sucking at her repeatedly, plunging his tongue deep. She tasted sweet and smelled like the two of them, and it was a heady fucking combination.

Peering up her body, he caught her staring down at him with hooded eyes, her teeth sinking into her bottom lip. "Fuck, you're gorgeous," he said.

Her eyes flared as if he'd caught her off guard. It made him wonder if he should back off of giving voice to the shit that popped into his head, except that she seemed to be all about cutting to the chase, too. And then she wiped his concern away. "You are, too."

Jesse slid his hand between her legs, stroking her with his fingers as she thrust into his touch.

"Please," she pleaded, the wet evidence of her need driving him wild.

But he wasn't hurrying this. "Taking my time, Tara. Remember?"

"Oh, God," she whimpered as he stroked through her arousal and sank one finger deep into her heat. And then he put his mouth back on her, because little had made him feel better in years than the way her body was shaking under his touch.

She'd said earlier that she feared she'd think this was all a dream come tomorrow, and Jesse was determined to make sure that didn't happen. He wanted to leave her muscles weak, her skin marked, her body absolutely spent from the pleasure she received at his hands. With his mouth. From his cock.

After this night, he wanted Tara to want to come back for more. Because he already knew, as fantastic as all this was, one taste, one time wasn't going to be enough. Not for him. Not when she looked at him with eyes so full of possibility, with none of the usual disappointment he was used to reading when people looked his way. Not when her moans and her screams and, hell, even her laughter told him that tonight at least, he was good enough.

For once in his damn life.

At thirty-seven, he'd had his share of women. But nothing serious. *Never* anything serious. For twenty years—from the second he'd graduated high school, left small-town Montana, and never looked back—he'd prioritized the military. After all, the career had cost him his family, so it sure as hell seemed like he should make it his priority. And then there was his work as a navy diver and EOD tech. Nothing had ever demanded Jesse's 24/7 focus like keeping his people safe in a job in which they were all one hand tremor away from dying in an explosion of pink mist. Which so many of them had.

So damn many.

Tara's hands went to Jesse's hair, forcing him out of his head, away from thoughts he didn't want to be having.

He went at her more hungrily, liking that she'd been able to chase the shit of his memories away. Liking being distracted. Being desired. Being touched. It drove him on. Made him flick and circle and suck her clit until she was squeezing his shoulders with her thighs and scratching his scalp with blunt fingernails. He added a second finger and fucked her as he sucked, his cock demanding friction he wasn't going to give it yet.

"God, Jesse, don't stop."

He spoke against where she was hot and wet. "Never. Not when I wanted you from the second you looked at me." The moment his mouth returned to her clit, her core went tight around his fingers.

"Oh, fu—" Her breath cut off as her whole body arched and her muscles pulsed where he was inside her. He licked her through the orgasm, his mouth moving on her clit until she cried out and grasped his face in her hands, forcing him to let up. "G-gonna kill me."

He grinned at her, then slowly crawled up her body, loving the way she looked at him—the way her eyes on his body made him feel. Strong and worthy. He settled in along the side of her, his hand lazily stroking over her belly.

Tara pushed up and kissed him full on the mouth. How something could feel grateful and possessive all at once, Jesse didn't know. But fuck if that wasn't exactly how it felt as her hand cupped his jaw, her mouth opened wide over his, and her tongue licked at his again and again. "You taste like me," she whispered.

Jesse groaned and pushed his hips into her thigh, an instinctive movement full of need that reminded him how fucking hard he still was. And then her hand grasped him through his jeans. She squeezed and stroked until he couldn't help but grind into her touch.

"My turn." She gave his shoulder a good shove, forcing him onto his back. Then she was undoing his jeans and stripping him bare. On her knees between his legs, she swept her hair all to one side then took his cock in hand.

Jesse wanted to watch, but the tightness of her grip moving over him had his head falling back against the bed and just giving in to the pure fucking decadence of it. Her hair spilling against his hip was all the warning he had before her mouth closed around his head and her tongue bathed over his length.

"Jesus, Tara," he rasped, bracing one arm under his head so he could watch. "Feels so good."

Those blue eyes flashed up at him at the same time that she sucked him deep, deeper. Her eyelids fell shut as she took him into her throat and held him there.

Jesse's hands flew to her hair, and he nearly hollered at the gut punch of pleasure. It was all he could do not to thrust his hips, especially when she began to move in a way that made his cock fuck even deeper into her throat. Just small, quick ups and downs that shoved him so hard toward orgasm that he wasn't sure how he held back.

"Christ, baby, I don't want to come yet," he said, his voice a raw scrape.

Slowly, she withdrew until her tongue just flicked at his tip. "I don't see a problem with that."

"C'mere." He looked his fill of her body moving over his, and then he wrapped his arms around her and pulled her close. "I want to be in you first."

She nodded, her face soft with arousal and something sweet that looked like affection. Or maybe that was him projecting his own messed-up state of mind. But then she looked away as she reached over to where his jeans were discarded on the edge of the bed. "Do you have another condom?"

"Fuck. No," he said. "Fuck."

She smiled and kissed his jaw, once, twice. "I'm happy to finish you with my mouth."

He tucked a long wave of hair behind her ear, and then rolled them until they lay side by side, one of his arms under her head, their legs tangled. "I want to hold you right here," he said, taking himself in hand. "So I can feel you against me when I get off."

Tara's gaze cut to where he was stroking himself between them, his fist bumping against her belly on the upstroke. Her bottom lip caught on her teeth before her tongue stroked over her lip, leaving a glossy streak. "God, that looks hot."

"Yeah?"

She squeezed her legs together, and the idea that he was arousing her again lanced white heat through his blood. "I could help." Her fingertips stroked at his balls, then she cupped him in a gentle squeeze.

"Can't make this last," he rasped.

"Don't try to," she said, tugging at his sack until he was clenching his teeth at the goodness of it all.

He tightened his grip and stroked himself faster. "Tara." Her name came out as a plea.

"Want to feel you on my skin." With that invitation on her tongue, she kissed him until he couldn't breathe and couldn't care.

And couldn't hold back. He groaned into the kiss as his cock jerked in his hand, and his cum lashed heat across his fingers and her belly. His heart a fucking freight train in his chest, he lay there completely obliterated.

"We should...probably clean up," he finally managed.

Tara curled into his side, and he hauled her in tighter with an arm around her shoulders. "I don't think I could move right now if I tried."

"Can barely talk," he said.

She chuckled, and her breath puffed against his chest. "Okay if I stay for a while?"

Stay as long as you want.

That was his gut-check of an internal reaction. Not that he voiced it. "O'course."

"Good." She heaved a deep breath and slid her knee up across his thighs.

It made him feel claimed. Like he belonged to her. Dangerous fucking feelings when neither thing was true. When he was claimed by no one and belonged nowhere. Not anymore.

All of which probably should've had him ushering her out of his bed. But no one had ever accused Jesse Anderson of making good choices. So he pulled Tara in tighter. And promised himself he wasn't going to fuck up or let anyone down.

Not this time.

* * * *

Tara had no idea where she was.

Or who she was with.

She lifted her head and looked up the hard masculine body on which she lay. Jesse. His hotel room. The single best night of sex of her life.

Oh. Oh, right.

She eased off the bed, but Jesse didn't move a muscle. And God he was gorgeous. Between his cock lying soft against his belly, the ink all down his arm, and the miles of lean muscle, his nudity was downright decadent. She could stand here all freaking night and never get bored taking in each new detail.

But her bladder had something to say about that. So Tara closed herself into the bathroom, careful to shut the door as quietly as she could. She did a double-take as she glanced at her reflection in the mirror.

Her hair was a hand-tousled wreck. Her lips appeared puffy. And her stomach still bore the dried evidence of Jesse's orgasm.

Girl, you look well fucked and then some.

She really, really did. And it was almost like she was looking at a stranger because Tara Hunter had never picked up a man at a bar in her whole life. Nor had sex the first night she'd met someone. Nor had orgasms so strong they left her breathless and boneless.

I really need to do this sort of thing more often.

A half-giddy, half-hysterical chuckle bubbled up, and she clapped a hand over her mouth. Hopefully, her sex high would get her through her first day on the new team tomorrow, because at this rate she'd be lucky to get three hours of sleep before her 7:30 AM all-hands meeting.

Tara cleaned herself up and used the toilet, then waited until the water stopped running inside the bowl before she opened the door.

Out in the room, Jesse lay sound asleep in the same position. Still freaking gorgeous. But she couldn't fully appreciate it just then because anxiety was digging its claws into her nervous system, making her second-guess her choice to drink and get so little sleep before her first day back on a diving team. And that made regret drop like a rock into her belly.

Because Tara needed to leave.

She gathered her clothes. Redressed. Stepped into her boots.

Jesse's phone had spilled from his coat pocket onto the floor by the suite's door. She grabbed it wondering if she could put her number into his contacts, and was pleased if a little surprised to find that it wasn't password protected.

She called her cell from his, then added herself as a contact.

Name: Tara Hunter

Mobile: 202-555-2341

Employer: Rick's Cafe

The Casablanca reference made her grin. But then she couldn't decide if it was stupid and awkward. Clearly she wasn't cool enough for super-hot one-night stands.

Rolling her eyes at herself, she placed his phone, still open to her contact profile, in the center of the little dining table so he would see it.

And then all there was to do was leave.

Giving Jesse a last look, she wondered how long it would be until she saw him again. *If* she saw him again. Because there was probably a difference between what people said in the heat of the moment, and what they actually did in the bright light of day and the reality of life.

And even if there was no next time, Tara wouldn't regret this. Ever since that cable had tried to separate her head from her shoulders, she'd realized that even the worst life could throw at you was better than not living at all.

Tara went for the door, wincing at how loudly the handle disengaged. Out in the hall, she did her best to make it close quietly, but as hotel doors were quite possibly one of the loudest things humankind had ever invented—which, when you really thought about it, made no freaking sense—there was only so much she could do.

She made for the elevator, the feeling that she was somewhere she didn't belong growing with each step and then, after she pushed the call button, with each second that passed until the elevator doors rolled open. Standing dead center, she told herself not to look over her shoulder, but she did it anyway, her imagination alive with the memory of Jesse pinning her in the corner while whispering sexy promises that he'd definitely kept.

It only took her ten minutes until she was standing in her own apartment—that was how close they lived to one another. At least temporarily.

If it wasn't for the delicious ache between her legs, she might've almost been able to believe the night hadn't happened. Which was why she crawled into bed without getting a shower. She didn't want to wash Jesse off her skin just yet. She wanted to wake up still smelling of him. Of them together.

Muttering at the stupidity of getting less than two hours of sleep the night before a new gig, she chugged a glass of water to flush the last of the alcohol from her system and set her alarm for six-fifteen. Then six-twenty. Then six-thirty, negotiating with herself that doing her wet hair in a braid would take less time than blow drying.

But then, of course, she couldn't fall asleep.

Because all she could think of was the flirting and the sex and all the times she'd laughed. And the sex. Plus the orgasms. Which just led her right back to the sex.

And Jesse.

She put the pillow over her face and shouted into the stuffing. Which obviously didn't help with the sleeping.

The last time she saw the clock, it was 5:25. Which meant her body was all kinds of unhappy when her alarm went off at 6:30.

Sitting on the edge of the bed, she scrubbed her face with her hands.

It was moments like this that her twelve years in the navy came in handy. Her body was well trained to push through without sleep or food, even in high-stress situations. Of course, that was before the accident had left her with a newfound anxiety and a fear of her work environment that she was still trying to fully overcome.

Heaving a deep breath, Tara got her butt up and into the shower.

Not only was today the first day working with a new diving team, she'd be the only woman on that team—which wasn't entirely unusual. But no way was she giving her fellow divers even one reason to think she wasn't as qualified and skilled as they were, or that she wouldn't have their six just like they'd have hers. Which meant she needed to get her head in the game and button her issues up tight.

Chapter 5

The headquarters of Commercial Marine Diving and Salvage wasn't much to look at, but it was part of what was making DC feel more and more like a place Tara could call home.

She parked her RAV4 in front of the white warehouse located at the marina near the Washington Navy Yard. It'd been about four months since she'd last been to CMDS. In the Mid-Atlantic, the main diving season was March through October, depending on the weather. During the off months, she'd worked as a diving instructor down in Florida for eight weeks, racking out at the townhouse of a friend from the navy who was deployed.

Instructor work was pure fun and low stress, and it'd been the perfect respite before getting back in the water on what were sure to be some more challenging projects.

Tara grabbed her duffle and made for the door. It was a lot warmer already this morning, warm enough that the thin snow covering that remained was melting off—which was good because water temps were already going to be freaking cold as it was.

She was both excited and nervous to see some familiar faces. Last year, she'd moved to DC in February and landed her position with CMDS in June, so she'd only worked half the season. Most of the rest of the team had worked together for years, and it'd taken a while before she'd felt like she really fit in. Now, she knew them and they knew her, and she'd be with them from day one.

All of which made *today* feel like the true beginning of her new post-naval career. One where she'd have the same respect and camaraderie that she'd built in the navy with a dozen years of diving experience under her belt—or, rather, under her neoprene dry suit.

The inside of HQ wasn't much more impressive than the outside. There was a small reception area with a few folding chairs, a coffee table covered in magazines, a coffee station, and, most importantly, Miss Delores sitting at the front desk.

"Tara Hunter, welcome back," Miss Delores said. She was the owner's wife, the firm's receptionist, and their logistics specialist— whatever the team needed, she made sure they had it.

"Hi, Mama D," Tara replied. The nickname still felt funny on her tongue, but it was what all the men on the team called her, and Tara thought the affection behind it was sweet. Not to mention, it was kinda accurate, too, because the older lady could both go Mama Bear when someone or something messed with the team, and she wasn't shy about mothering them when someone was being difficult or stubborn or otherwise hadn't squared their shit away.

And since Tara's own mom had died right after high school, she'd liked Delores right away.

"How was Florida?" Mama D came around from behind her desk to give Tara a hug. She was a petite lady in her fifties, with a sun tan and freckles that spoke of a lifetime spent out on the water.

"It was heaven. And fun. More like a vacation than work."

Holding her by the arms, Mama D smiled, her gaze running over Tara's face like she was making sure Tara was okay. "That sounds real good, hon. I'm glad. Well, a few of the boys are already back there. And I brought in some Dunkin' for y'all so you better go before they eat all the good donuts."

Tara laughed. Both at the lady calling her teammates 'boys' when most of them were older than Tara, and at the reality that you had to act fast when free food was available around here. "Oh, damn, I better hurry then."

With a wave, Tara hiked her duffle higher on her shoulder and pushed through the swinging door that led past some offices to the conference room where they held their all-hands meetings.

Commercial diving teams varied in size, depending on their members' credentials and skill sets, and the four men she found already gathered around the donuts probably represented most of the team. "Hey, save some for me," Tara said, smiling as everyone turned around and called out greetings.

One by one, she said hello and returned hugs. There was Delores's husband, Boone Macon, owner of CMDS and their supervisor on all their diving ops. Next to him, there was Jud Taylor, another navy guy who was one of their primary working divers who handled the brunt of the team's underwater work. Together with herself, Bobby Flannery was one of the standby divers who also doubled as bellman—operator of an underwater bell platform. Finally, Mike Henson was a former Coastie who handled all things tech, equipment, and systems—without whom their underwater work was neither possible nor safe. He'd been a new addition at the end of last diving season, so Tara didn't know him well.

"You ready to get wet?" Jud teased. As he always did. Incessantly.

She smirked as she grabbed a frosted donut. "You sure you want to harass the diver responsible for rescuing your cowboy ass when you get in trouble?"

"I like to live dangerously," he said with a wink as he passed her a truce in the form of a perfectly made cup of coffee.

"You're forgiven," she said as she accepted it and took a sip.

Boone gathered some files and sat with his breakfast at the far end of the conference table. "We're just waiting on Jefferson and Anderson and then we'll get started."

"I'm here," George Jefferson said as he walked into the room wearing a big smile. "Now the party can start." A round of singing—of the theme song from *The Jeffersons*, naturally—greeted the man who assisted Mike on all things systems but, more importantly, served as their medical tech.

George shook his head at the lot of them as he dumped his duffle, put his coat around the back of the chair, and waited for them to finish, which didn't take long since they only seemed to know the first few lines of lyrics. "After all this time, you'd think you people would've learned the words to that damn song." Laughter filled the room, and a new chorus of sarcastic barbs got flung back and forth, the kind that revealed what good friends they all really were.

This was the kind of community Tara had enjoyed in the navy, and it meant a lot to her to find it here, too. Everyone was still catching up when she took her seat, but then she popped back up to snag a second donut because, after not sleeping, sugar was pretty much life.

As the others found their own seats, Mama D's voice echoed from out in the hall. "And here's where the team meets. Boone and the others will show you around from here," she said as she stepped into the doorway.

A tall man with dark hair shook her hand. "Thank you, ma'am."

Ooh, those good manners aren't going to last long around here, Tara thought as she sipped at her coffee, eager to meet their newest teammate—and glad to not *be* the newbie this time.

And then the man turned around.

Jesse?

Jesse!

Coffee got stuck in Tara's throat, because of course it did, and then she couldn't stop coughing.

Which was when Jesse's gaze swung from George and Mike, whose hands he'd just been shaking, to her. He blanched.

"You okay there, T?" Flannery asked.

"Yeah," she said around a choking gasp. "Wrong hole."

"That's what she said!" at least three of her asshole teammates guffawed, sending everyone into hysterics. Everyone except for her and Jesse.

Jesse. Jesse *Anderson*. Apparently the new working diver on her team.

Heat roared over Tara's face, which of course brought more teasing her way, but it was better that everyone thought her embarrassment was over the stupid softball teasing opportunity she'd tossed them than because she'd screwed their new teammate eight hours ago.

The coughing fit finally passed, but still her heart raced and her face burned and those two freaking donuts turned sour and heavy in her belly. How could this be happening?

How could this be happening?

She watched in not a little horror as he made his way around the table, shaking the men's hands and getting closer to having to say…something…to her. Was he going to make it clear they knew each other? Did she want him to?

Naturally, her nerdy engineer's brain began drawing up pro and con lists. On the side of acknowledging their familiarity was that it would be super hella awkward to have to pretend they were strangers, and it would also kinda suck to deny the connection they'd shared, when she felt like it'd been so thoroughly based on honesty and openness. And of all the things they'd talked about, how the heck hadn't they covered their jobs?

It was a full-on head-desk moment.

But on the side of *hello, stranger, you must be new around these parts* was her gut-deep embarrassment at having slept with a co-worker and the other men maybe figuring that out.

Next to her now, Jesse was shaking Flannery's hand, which meant it was her turn to try to act like a normal human being. Whatever that meant in this situation, she didn't have a single clue. Especially when Jesse was so freaking hot. Like, you'd think her body would be in too great a state of panic to notice that. But nooooo. Of course not. Instead, it was like her blood and her skin were *attuned* to the man, with her scalp remembering the feel of his hand and her clit remembering the suction of his mouth and her core remembering the satisfying fullness of his cock.

Oh, Jesus, Tara, don't think about his cock.

And naturally that was the moment he moved to stand in front of her. Tara stood to return his handshake. Their gazes collided as their fingers touched, and she thought she saw in his dark eyes the roiling ball of conflicting emotions she felt herself.

"Hey," he said. And with just that one word in that familiar deep voice, she felt the memory of his arms around her waist and his chin settle on her head, the way it had last night. "Jesse Anderson. Nice to meet you."

The words kinda hit her like a gut punch. Which was ridiculous when she'd just been debating pretending like she didn't know him either. "Uh, hey, Jesse," she managed. "Tara Hunter. Welcome to the team."

"Welcome to DC."

"You really know how to show a guy a good time."

"Thanks," he said, while her brain ran a repeated loop of *Oh, baby Jesus, help me.*

He held onto her hand a beat longer than felt natural, so she withdrew. His brows cranked down just the littlest bit, and her mind unhelpfully replayed another conversation from last night.

"Did it get awkward?"

"Not yet."

Dear God, the awkward achievement had definitely been unlocked now. Like, Defcon-1-level awkward even.

As Jesse moved to greet Boone, Tara sank back into her chair and attempted to plaster a neutral expression on her face that she feared probably looked more like Edvard Munch's *The Scream.*

On his way to grab some breakfast and a seat further down the table, Jesse moved behind her chair again, and the ripple of awareness that tingled across her back made her feel like she was a compass and he was

True North.

As Boone started introducing some of the contracts he'd already signed for the season, Tara could barely focus on the words coming out of the man's mouth.

And that was the biggest problem of all in this whole goddamned mess.

Tara *did not* tolerate distractions at work. *Could not.*

Not when she'd nearly died in the water. Not when it'd taken her so many therapy sessions, not to mention the alternate therapy of Warrior Fight Club, to feel confident getting back into the water. And not when she sometimes still struggled with anxiety at the mere prospect of it.

But Jesse...

She fought the urge to peer down the table at him.

Jesse Anderson was definitely a distraction.

Now Tara just had to figure out what she was going to do about it.

Chapter 6

Unfuckingbelievable.

That was the tenor of Jesse's thoughts as he spent the morning sitting ten feet away from his one-night stand.

From Tara.

The woman he'd hoped to see again.

The woman who'd snuck out of his hotel room in the middle night without leaving her number.

The woman who was one of his new freaking teammates. Apparently.

His gaze drifted from the notes he was taking to Boone at the head of the table, and then traitorously to Tara. She'd done her hair in a thick rope of a braid that hung down her back and was dressed simply in a navy blue sweatshirt and jeans. And he found her every bit as beautiful as he had last night. When he'd fucked her against the wall. Then shattered her with his mouth. Then watched her take every inch of him down her throat.

For fuck's sake.

There was no *apparently* about it.

That woman was now his colleague. And before he'd even had his first day on the job, he'd already gone and fucked something up.

Goddamnit, Jesse.

Anger and resentment pounded through his veins. Anger at himself, for *always* falling short. Anger at the universe, for never once giving him a break—and gee didn't the pity party make him feel even more awesome.

And anger at her, too, if he was honest. For making him think something else was possible, for running out without a word, for being here now.

Her being on the team wasn't a fair thing for him to be mad about. He knew that. And he'd force himself over it post haste because he could be a professional. And because he couldn't risk doing another thing that might blow the fresh start he'd been hoping to make here.

Still, the whole snafu sucked some major ass. But sometimes it was just your turn to embrace the suck.

A little after twelve, Boone wrapped up the all-hands meeting, and Delores surprised them by bringing in platters of submarine sandwiches, salads, and chips.

"Donuts and subs all in one day?" George asked, grabbing the tray from the older lady's hands. "Best be careful, or Jud will just move his ass in here and then you'll never get rid of him."

Jud nodded. "True, but I'm awesome. Anybody would be lucky to have me."

Tara snorted, and the sound drew some appreciative chuckles.

"I think you just got shot down without T actually having to say a real word, champ," Bobby said.

"You wound me, Tara. Wound me bad," Jud said in what Jesse guessed what a Texas accent. The guy threw her a wink when she rolled her eyes, and hell if a tendril of jealousy didn't try to curl around Jesse's spine.

"You'll live," she said with a smirk. "And if not, George will consider resuscitating you."

As more laughter rose up, everyone began fixing plates and chatting. Jesse couldn't help but keep an ear tuned toward Tara, and he found himself admiring the rapport she had with the men here, and the way she gave as good as she got. It couldn't be easy to be the only woman on a team of mostly prior military men, which made him feel even shittier for resenting finding her here. He was the outsider looking in on all their inside jokes. She was the one who belonged.

He put a turkey sub on his plate and froze. If the men were mostly vets...

Jesse looked across the table at Tara, and his gaze landed on the scar on her throat. Did that mean she was a veteran, too? And now he was really wondering what the hell had happened to her.

Each new thing about her intrigued him.

Which had him back to being pissed off again, because if they were colleagues they probably shouldn't also be *more*. And, *goddamnit*, he'd been hoping that last night might have the chance to be something more.

Maybe not forever. Maybe not even a relationship. But more than just one night.

Tara did a doubletake when she caught him staring, and Jesse clenched his teeth together and dropped his gaze to the pasta salad, which he mechanically scooped onto his plate.

And then they were all sitting down again and shooting the shit. Jud was the one who finally pulled Jesse into the conversation. "So, Jesse, where you joining us from, man?"

He cleared his throat. "Was stationed at Coronado before I retired."

"Aw, San Diego's beautiful," Jud said. "DC sucks by comparison."

Jesse nodded. "From Montana, originally, so I'm used to winters, too. But, yeah, I'm not sure anywhere can beat San Diego's weather."

Jud wiped his mouth with the back of his hand. "So what was your rating?"

"SPECWAR," Jesse said, referring to the Special Warfare community that had a lot of its commands at the Coronado base. "Started out ND and then moved on to EOD." It was his experience in those jobs as a navy diver and explosives and ordnance disposal technician that had landed him this job. This chance to do better.

Jud's eyebrows rose. "EOD? Damn. So if I see *you* running, I guess I better catch up."

Jesse grinned. "Roger that."

Jud nodded at Tara. "T and I were both SEABEEs. I was at Gulfport, but she was at Little Creek."

Jesse's gaze cut to Tara, surprise filling his gut. The SEABEEs were the navy's construction force, which sounded way more mundane than it was, by a lot. They were responsible for a whole host of dangerous jobs, including building forward operating bases in unstable areas, handling rescue and salvage operations, and supporting civilian authorities during natural disasters. And those stationed at Little Creek, the nickname for the Joint Expeditionary Base in Virginia Beach, provided combat and logistics support to the SPECWAR and SPECOPS communities there, including the SEALS. He'd worked with some of the SEABEEs stationed likewise at Coronado, and he knew they were badass and often scary brilliant to boot.

Tara arched a single brow, not much, but just enough that he noticed. And something in those blue eyes seemed to be asking him if he had something to say.

Hell, yeah, he did. *Many* things. Starting with, *How can you think you're not interesting?* Like he'd been able to get her off his mind before learning all of this.

She looked down at her plate when she grabbed some chips, but Jesse had the distinct feeling that her intent had been more about breaking the way he'd held her gaze.

And it made his desire to feel her eyes on him that much stronger.

Damn it all to hell.

And even though he joined in the rest of the conversation—learning that Boone and Delores had worked together as long as they'd known one another, and that Bobby was from Boston, and that Mike was still in the Coast Guard reserves—part of Jesse's brain remained fixated on Tara.

Her pretty face. Her gorgeous body. Her intriguing past.

He wanted it all.

But now that they would be working together—two members on a team of seven—he had no idea how that was going to be possible.

* * * *

Tara knew hiding out in the women's locker room long enough to ensure that Jesse had left was a chickenshit move, but she did it anyway. Because *bockbockbock*.

All day, she'd caught him sneaking glances her way, and the expressions he'd worn had ranged from merely curious to clearly unhappy to, on at least one occasion, downright hungry. None of which she wanted to further explore while she was at work. For crap's sake.

And her cowardice had paid off, apparently, because Boone and Mama D were the only ones still there when she came into the reception area.

"Oh, I'm sorry," Tara said, catching the older couple in a kiss.

"Don't be," Mama D said with a sassy wink. "We've been married forever and a day, but we still can't get enough of each other. Isn't that right, Boone?"

Her boss looked significantly less comfortable with the turn of the conversation. "Sure, Dee."

Tara chuckled, her feelings more in line with Boone on this one. "Well, I'll just say good night, then."

"Be careful in all that rain," Mama D said, throwing Tara a wave as she made for the front door.

The rainfall on the warehouse's metal roof had been obvious for the past hour, but Tara didn't realize just how hard it was coming down until she peered outside. Huge puddles had absorbed the last of the snow and now covered the ground. She hesitated on the threshold for just a minute, then made a run for it. She was drenched by the time she closed herself inside her car, and her shoes were soaked through to her feet.

The weather was supposed to be crappy most of this week, which was going to wreak havoc on their schedule if it stayed this bad, all of which was just part of the reality of doing work outside and underwater.

Pushing wet tendrils of hair back from her face, she started the car and eased out of the lot. Even set on high, her windshield wipers barely kept up with the deluge as she drove down the marina's service road for the main entrance. Luckily, it was only about a fifteen-minute drive back to her place, though rush hour was undoubtedly going to be a mucked-up mess.

The only saving grace was that she hadn't taken the Metro this morning. Normally, she didn't mind the walk between the closest stop and CMDS, but in this it would've been miserable.

She grimaced when she passed someone walking along the marina's main drive in the rain, head and shoulders hunched. *Poor guy.* And then she realized who it was.

Jesse.

For just a split second, she hesitated. Shaking her head at herself, she pulled to the curb, because the fact that she'd even debated whether to offer him a ride—like she would for anyone else on the team—showed precisely how screwed up this whole situation was.

She opened the window on the passenger's door and called out as he came alongside her car. "Get in."

Jesse did a doubletake, and then he hesitated, too.

She waved at him. "Come on, get in."

He braced those big hands on the opening of the window. Hands that had handled bombs, apparently. She'd worked a lot of years with guys like him, long enough to know that navy EODs earned the prestige universally attributed to their rating. They were undeniably brave, incredibly calculated and precise, and often loners. She'd once heard someone describe them as being as cool as jet pilots, with the hands of a heart surgeon. In her experience, that was pretty dead on.

Like she might pose him some danger, he leaned down slowly until he was peering at her through the window. His hair was so wet it appeared jet black, and rain drops covered his face and caught on his eyelashes.

He was…almost unbearably gorgeous.

"Get in," she said again.

"I shouldn't."

Something in his voice made her belly do a little flip. "You're soaked. And it's not out of my way. Obviously."

"Tara—"

"Jesse, it's a *ride.*"

He heaved a sigh. "It's fine. I'm already wet anyway—"

"I'm almost certain you would've outranked me, but I'm going to issue this order anyway. Sailor, get in the damn car."

The next thing she knew, he was sitting next to her, his big body making the car feel small.

She used the control on her door to close his window and watched as he dragged a hand down his face.

"See, that wasn't hard."

The look he threw her felt like he'd taken a blow torch to her blood. For a moment, she was totally confused by the intensity of it, and then it hit her. *Oh. Oh!* Her gaze dropped to his lap, which was covered by his coat, of course. Just as quickly, she glanced back to his dark eyes.

"I think you should drive."

She let out a shaky breath. "Uh, right. Good. Driving now."

They caught the red light at the main intersection out of the marina. While they sat there, only the drumming of the rain and the *thunk-thunk* of the windshield wipers between them, about a hundred things competed to be said. But Tara held her tongue because Jesse was radiating *back off* loud enough that he might as well have just said it out loud.

Chancing a glance at him, she found him peering out his window. The hard angles of his face in profile appeared even more stark, more masculine. God, more appealing. Tara sighed.

The light finally turned green.

They didn't say a word until they turned onto the street that led past her apartment to his hotel.

"I'll drop you at your place," she said.

"I can walk from your building."

"But why—"

"You've done enough."

She heard the words, but there was something in the tone she couldn't discern. Something that made her pull into her garage instead of passing it by like she'd intended. Residents had assigned parking spaces, so she went down two floors until she came to the reserved spot for apartment 1120.

Tara cut the engine and turned to him. "What does that mean?"

Those dark eyes cut to her. "What?"

"That I've done enough."

His mouth opened and closed two times. With a shrug, he finally said, "Today would've been awkward no matter what, but I guess it must've been even more uncomfortable for you given that you never intended to see me again."

Tara blinked. "Huh?"

His brows cranked down. "You left without a word."

Now her gaze was the one narrowing. "I left because it was getting close to morning and I had a six AM wake-up. I didn't know whether to wake you. So instead I called my phone with yours and created a contact." She arched a brow.

Like there was possibly a snake in his pocket, he slowly retrieved the cell. Thumbed it awake. Opened the phone app. She knew the moment he saw the outgoing call at nearly 4 AM to 'Tara Hunter *mobile*' because his hand fell slack in his lap.

"Shit."

"That about covers it." She pushed out of the car and slammed the door. Then paced behind the RAV4 until he finally got his annoyingly hot ass out and faced her. "If you think today was any easier for me, you're wrong."

"Okay," he said, looking appropriately chagrinned.

"That's it? Just…'okay'?" She braced her hands on her hips.

"What else do you want me to say?"

"I…I don't even know. But this…" She gestured back and forth between them. "This is exactly why this situation is a problem. You were mad at me today because you thought I'd ghosted on you. You didn't see me as one of your teammates, you saw me as a woman you'd slept with. Which is another problem. Because if you don't think it's challenging being the only woman on this team, you'd be wrong again."

"I understand, Tara, and I agree. I get that last night was a mistake."

The word hit her like a gut punch, even though she'd been mulling whether it'd been a mistake or not herself. She just hadn't been able to reduce what'd happened between them to that. It had just been too perfect, too...*real.* Though he obviously didn't feel the same way or have the same hesitation. "Okay," she managed.

"For the record, I absolutely see you as one of my teammates. Because you *are* one of my teammates. And I'll treat you the same as everyone else."

She nodded. "Good. Because I don't want any distractions at work."

"Fair enough," he said, an edge to his words.

On a sigh, she turned. "Elevator's over here."

They crossed the garage side by side, their footsteps and the hum of the ventilation the only sounds. She pushed the call button, her stomach heavy with a weird falling sensation at how different this moment was from the last time they'd ridden in an elevator together.

All of which had been a mistake. Apparently.

The doors rolled open, and she stepped in and pressed the buttons for both the lobby and her floor. He followed, standing next to her as the doors eased shut.

This felt...so crappy. She hated it.

And that made her determined. "Since last night was such a mistake, it shouldn't happen again."

The bell dinged. The doors slid open.

Jesse gave a single nod. "Fine."

And then he was gone and Tara was all alone again—and not at all sure that their conversation had done a single thing that would make work tomorrow any less awkward.

Chapter 7

You fucked up again.

It'd been nearly twenty-four hours since Jesse had left Tara in an elevator, and that one thought still hadn't stopped running through his head. Because he almost couldn't have handled the conversation with her any worse.

Thank God they'd both been so busy all day getting their asses kicked by the chop of the Chesapeake Bay. The team's first job was assisting an offshore wind company with an underwater survey of a planned wind farm about seventeen nautical miles off the coast of Ocean City. The company had apparently done part of the survey last summer, but the project kept getting held up by political wrangling in the state government. Now it seemed the wind farm was back on again, and the company was under the gun to finish the survey this week, assuming the weather cooperated.

But before they could do any of that, they had to get there.

First thing this morning, they'd departed DC on CMDS's diving support vessel *Going Deep*, lovingly nicknamed "the GD DSV" by his teammates. But the Chesapeake Bay could be a nasty piece of water if the wind, weather, and tides weren't right, as was the case today. And the Delaware Bay wasn't much better.

Jesse heaved a deep breath as they finally passed the ferry terminal at Lewes, Delaware, and came around into the Atlantic Ocean. They'd hit Ocean City in a little over an hour if the calmer seas held.

He'd been wet and cold for the entirety of the day-long trip, but still it felt good to be back out on the water. His sea legs under him again, the smell of salt air in his nose. Of course, he would've been able to enjoy it all even more if he hadn't made a tricky situation worse with Tara.

When he'd awakened yesterday to find himself alone, he'd looked for a note from Tara. Not finding one had been a total gut check, because it cast doubts over everything he'd thought his night with her had been about. It hadn't occurred to him to check his phone because apparently he was an idiot who'd been too pissed, disappointed, and late for work to think clearly.

And that wasn't even the worst of it.

The momentary flash of hurt on Tara's face when he'd called their night together a mistake still had him feeling two feet tall. He'd thought that was what she'd concluded, so he'd said it first because the thought of hearing her call him a mistake was more than he could stomach.

"You could've done so much more, been so much more. The navy is a mistake, Jesse. One you'll have to live with now."

His dad's twenty-year-old words rang in his ears as he watched lights twinkle along the shoreline in one picturesque beach town after another. On a sigh, he made his way to the bridge, where he found Boone, Jud, Bobby, and Tara.

Jesse joined in the small talk as the lights of Ocean City finally came into view, and though things with Tara seemed normal and they were both hanging out with the team, none of their exchanges were directly with the other. And that sucked because it revealed there was still some weirdness between them, just one more piece of evidence that he was really fucking bad at this—*this* including everything from living up to his parents' expectations to protecting his EOD techs to basic goddamned human interaction. Apparently.

He was grateful when pulling into the marina gave him something else to think about. All hands were on deck as they docked, secured the DSV, and checked in with the harbor master so they could refuel. It would be their last night with a hot, leisurely meal and sleeping in a soft bed on dry land for a few days, and Jesse was looking forward to both as they made their way to Captain Joe's, which was famous for its Maryland crab cakes.

The restaurant was one of those places that appeared to have been there for decades, with weathered wood paneling, colored-glass light fixtures, and a bar surrounded by old timers. The team pulled some tables together in an otherwise quiet corner and settled in.

As was a CMDS tradition, Boone treated them to a couple of pitchers of beer and raised his glass in a toast. "To going deep and getting it done."

"Here, here!" everyone called as they raised and clinked their frosty mugs.

Jesse took a long pull of the cold beer, relishing the malt on his tongue.

Jud made the next toast. "And here's to welcoming Jesse to the island of misfit toys, otherwise known as this team."

Laughing, everyone raised their glasses again. Including Tara, who gave him a little smile when their mugs touched. He was glad for it, but definitely didn't know what he'd possibly done to earn it.

"Thanks," Jesse said, pulling his gaze away from her. "If y'all are misfits, I should fit right in."

"That's the spirit," Jud said, clapping him on the back.

The next hour passed over a fantastic meal and storytelling about the stupid shit various team members had done over the years, including Tara being famous for singing Alvin and the Chipmunks songs after decompressing from dives deep enough to require mixed air—a mixture of oxygen and helium.

Jesse grinned at her. "I can't wait to hear that."

Tara shrugged. The wind had pulled more than a few tendrils of curls down from her braid, and they framed her face so perfectly. "It's pretty epic, honestly."

"I bet it is," he said, thinking that everything he'd learned—and experienced—where she was concerned had been pretty epic. Which was going to make working and sleeping in close quarters interesting for the rest of the week. But at least it didn't seem like she wanted to stab him with her fork, so he was counting that as a win.

Hell, Jesse Anderson had learned to take wins where he could find them.

Before long, they were checking into a no-frills hotel close to the marina. Everyone begged off hanging out given their five AM underway time. After two days of not sleeping great, Jesse wanted nothing more than to collapse into bed. Boone randomly passed out key cards, and they made for the elevator as a group.

The doors opened at the second floor, and Boone and George got out with a wave.

"See you on the flip side," Jud said when he and Bobby stepped out onto the third floor, leaving him, Mike, and Tara behind.

Jesse flipped open the little envelope that held his key. Room 401.

The elevator doors rolled open on four, and he and Tara made for the opening at the same time. Hiking his duffle up higher on his shoulder, he gestured for her to go first.

"'Night, Mike," she called.

"'Night," the man replied. Jesse threw a wave over his shoulder.

He turned left. So did Tara.

She threw a skeptical look over her shoulder, one eyebrow arched.

Jesse couldn't help but chuckle. "Promise I'm not following you."

"Didn't think you were," she said.

They passed a bunch of rooms, yet both of them were still heading toward the end of the hall.

Tara looked over her shoulder again. "What room are you in?" she asked, her tone a mix of exasperation and humor.

"Uh, four oh one?"

"Oh, for crap's sake."

She muttered it under her breath, but he heard it all the same. "Why? Where are you?"

Stopping in front of 403, she peered up at him. "This is me."

There was only one door left in the hallway—the room right next to hers. *His* room. "Guess we're destined to be neighbors."

Her gaze went from his eyes to his mouth to the floor. "I guess. Well, good night." She turned toward her door.

Jesse swallowed hard, because her gaze had been hungry, and it'd left his body hard and wanting. "G'night," he managed, forcing his feet to keep moving. This was work. And Tara was a colleague. That was all she could be.

All she *wanted* to be. She'd made that clear.

He stuck his card in the slot.

"Hey, Jesse?"

His gaze whipped toward her, and his heart was a sudden bass drum in his chest. "Yeah?"

"Just try not to throw any wild parties over there or anything." A ball-busting smile played around her mouth. A mouth he'd tasted. And that had tasted him. Jesus.

"Shit, T," he said, liking everyone's nickname for her. "The DJ's supposed to be here in like five fucking minutes."

For a split second, her eyes went wide, and then she smirked. "Smart ass."

"Uh huh, but I got you. For just a second, you fell for it. Admit it." This teasing between them was good. Natural. Maybe he hadn't fucked things up too bad after all.

Her expression went soft, almost wistful. She nodded. "Yeah, I guess I did fall for it. 'Night." Then she was gone, closed inside her room, the door locking mechanism clicking loudly between them.

Jesse was left standing there, half certain her parting words had been about more than just his joke. And those rocks took up residence in his gut once again.

* * * *

Tara had made a grave, grave mistake.

Except she didn't realize it right away.

It took her not one, but halfway into a *second* movie starring Keanu Reeves to realize that she'd spent her night with one incredibly sexy, tall, dark, and brooding loner with an air of hurt around him…to avoid knocking on the door of another man with damn similar traits.

"That wasn't even subtle, *id*," she said as she pushed her computer off her lap and onto the mattress—paused at a scene where Keanu went down on his sorta love interest like a man who'd skipped way too many meals.

Which had Tara remembering that Jesse had looked the same freaking way. Big shoulders spreading her thighs wide. Hands holding her down. Mouth ravenous against her skin. Dark eyes absolutely alive with lust.

Jesus. And now she was sweating and horny—not necessarily in that order. And the object of *her* lust was way, *way* too close. As in, just on the other side of the wall right behind her headboard. Where he needed to stay.

Because she was mad at him. And they were co-workers now. Annnd awkwardness.

Well, she wasn't really mad at him anymore. The day spent on the *Going Deep*, hands and mind at work, had helped. A lot. Because he was on her team now, and he was a hard worker, more than competent and conscientious, too. She respected all of that. So she'd determined to let everything he'd said go. Not for his benefit, but for hers. Having nearly died, she didn't want to make time in her life for anger and resentment.

By the time dinner had ended, Tara had felt like the weirdness was finally dissipating between them.

At least, it had been until fate had made them wall-sharing neighbors. *Thanks for nothing, Holiday Inn.*

Huffing, she pushed out of bed, went to the bathroom, and performed her nighttime routine, hoping it would chill out her libido. Except, nope. Toothbrushing versus horniness—no surprise, but horny won.

Tara doublechecked the locks on the door and shut out all the lamps, leaving her laptop to cast the only light in the room. She slipped between the sheets and reached to close it. Oh, she'd just watch the oral sex scene one more time.

Da-amn, Keanu.

Yeah, okay, that didn't help her situation at all.

Crap, Mama needs some porn.

She put the name of her favorite site into the navigation bar, and soon a pornucopia of sex acts filled her screen. She scrolled through a few pages and then finally succumbed to searching: *up against a wall.*

By this point, she was totally judging herself, but some things couldn't be helped.

And then, oh baby, she found one that looked perfect. Dark-haired man. Woman with long brown hair. Up against a wall.

Tara went to click play and then it occurred to her.

Shared. Wall.

Yikes. Right.

On a grimace, she made a dash for her earbuds, and then she was back in bed again, hand roaming over her body as her eyes drank in the unfolding scene.

It started with the couple making out against the wall just inside their house, like they hadn't been able to get further than the front door before *needing* each other. They kissed deeply, hungrily, only parting to shed clothes in a messy heap. And then the man put the woman on her knees, her back against the wall, and used her mouth in a way that made it impossible for Tara to resist sliding her fingers between her legs.

She was already wet. The friction of her fingers was so good she had to close her eyes at the sheer pleasure of it. But in her mind's eye, she saw Jesse there, peering up her body as he ate her out.

Her eyes flashed open again as she tried to force her brain to concentrate on the man and woman on the screen. The man pulled the woman up, ripped her panties, and lifted one of her thighs into the crook of his elbow. And then he guided his cock inside of her, both of them groaning and cursing.

Tara's fingers moved in harder, faster circles. God, she needed this. Needed him.

She clenched her eyes at the thought, but the couple's moans made her look again.

The man pulled out and spun the woman to face the wall, and then he grabbed her hips and buried himself deep. The woman cried out so loud it was nearly a scream.

And the scene was so perfectly reminiscent of what'd happened with Jesse, that so did Tara. She slapped her free hand over her mouth as the orgasm wracked through her so hard that she couldn't stop trembling. Her fingers circled her clit again and again, drawing out the explosive sensations until every one of Tara's muscles had gone taut and tense.

A full minute later, occasional tremors made her shake like she'd caught a shiver. Her whole body went limp as exhaustion absolutely swamped her. She tugged out her earbuds and closed her laptop. Stumbled in the darkness to use the bathroom again. Collapsed completely satisfied into bed.

Satisfied enough that she could avoid thinking about the fact that just her *memory* of Jesse Anderson had given her one of the best orgasms of her life.

Chapter 8

"Hey, wait for me!"

Jesse's gaze cut to his right, and he found Tara walking toward him, fresh-faced and smiling, her hair pulled back in a tight braid. She wore a long, baggy navy sweatshirt over her black thermal undersuit.

"Hey," he managed, holding the elevator door for her—while trying not to think about the fact that he'd heard her cry out last night. Since he'd borne witness to her orgasms before, he knew exactly what he'd heard. He would've put money on it.

She thanked him as she joined him in the elevator. Jesse leaned against the side wall, because that was literally as far away from her as he could get in the ten-by-ten box in which they were once again trapped.

Tara smirked at him. "I feel like we ride in a lot of elevators together."

Jesse nearly swallowed his tongue. At her cheek. At her addressing the elephant in the room. At how fucking happy she seemed at oh dark hundred, and with probably not much more sleep than he'd had himself. "I've noticed."

Her sleep last night was unfortunately something he knew about firsthand because he hadn't been able to sleep either. He'd been up late reading, chiding himself for the fact that he was going to feel like shit in the morning if he didn't get some shut-eye. Which was why he'd still been awake at 12:15 AM to hear it—the unmistakable sound of Tara's pleasure from probably three feet away. Close enough that, had the wall not been there, he would've been able to reach out and touch her.

And fuck if that wasn't exactly what he'd wanted to do.

Her ecstasy in his ear, it'd been so damn tempting. He'd literally stumbled out of bed, his mind already carrying his feet out of his room to pound on the door to hers. But he'd said they were a mistake. And she'd said nothing should happen between them again.

So he hadn't touched Tara. He'd touched himself. He'd shoved down his boxers, braced a hand on the fucking wall they shared, and jacked himself so hard and fast that he'd gone to his knees.

The image in his head the whole time? The way she'd looked when she'd come while his mouth sucked her off.

The thing that kept him awake for another hour? Wondering if there was any possibility that she'd come with the same memory in mind.

"Sleep okay?" she asked.

Jesse chuckled at the ridiculousness of their situation. "Okay enough."

"Ugh, I hear that." She tilted her head to one side, then the other, obviously trying to work out a kink. Her stretches gave him a close-up view of her scar, making him realize how deep the cut must've been. God, she'd been lucky to survive whatever had caused her injury.

"You okay?" he asked.

"Yeah, just…." She shrugged as the doors opened onto the lobby. The rest of the team was congregated there waiting, everyone in various types of thermals, and a round of greetings rose up as they stepped out, leaving Jesse curious about what Tara had been about to say.

Before long, they'd made their way to the *Going Deep*, finished supplying it for the trip, and were getting underway with no more chance to talk privately—probably a good thing, all things considered.

"Goood morning, Atlantic Ocean!" Jud called out, standing out in the light rain with his head back and his arms held wide, then he joined everyone on the bridge wearing a big smile.

Jesse looked at the guy with whom he'd be doing a lot of his underwater work. George laughed. "Jud's one of those annoying morning people."

"No shit," Jesse said, chuckling. But truth be told, excitement was filling his gut, too. It'd been too long since he'd last been in the water. In a way, he felt like he was coming home, which was a refreshingly good thing to feel.

About an hour later, they were at the edge of the survey site, a little over seventeen nautical miles offshore. In the rainy distance, they could just make out the silhouette of the Atlantic Wind Energy ship with whom they were working. They dropped anchor and made for what Jud referred to as the war room.

Located just behind the bridge, the room was part onboard conference room, part mission control. A bank of monitors lined one side, which would allow them to see multiple reports from their dive computers and any digital surveying they did.

"We're gonna touch base with the AWE team and then come up with our game plan," he said, making contact with the other ship. He put the receiver to his mouth. "This is the DVS *Going Deep*. Over."

The captain of the other ship introduced himself, and then both team leaders took a moment to introduce the entirety of their crews.

As both teams enumerated the plans and challenges, Jesse felt—for the first time in a long time—that he was right where he was supposed to be. On the water. In his element. Doing things he knew he was good at doing.

The company owned a lease for the potential installation of sixty turbines, and they still had a quarter of the area to survey. So they carved up the remaining area into two zones, with CMDS handling Zone 1, with waters ranging from fifty-five to eighty-five feet deep, and AWE handling the deeper waters of Zone 2.

All there was left to do was kit up—and Jud was up first. Because of maximum diving time limits, Jesse and Jud would be taking turns and diving in cycles—one of them on the bottom while the other rested on the surface until they off-gassed enough to dive again.

Tara served as Jud's tender, assisting him with dressing in the company's black and yellow neoprene dry suit. As Jesse checked the valves on his own suit, he watched the two of them work and shook his head at Jud, because the guy just couldn't resist joking around with and teasing her. She gave as good as she got, though, and clearly was more than able to take care of herself. And it made Jesse like her even more. Made him feel even more at home, if he was honest. Because even though not everyone on their team was prior military, their shit-talking had the same feeling of camaraderie, the same sense that people had your back as being in the navy.

Once Jud was fully kitted, he waited on the diving stage to allow Mike to perform a series of systems checks. Tara shed her sweatshirt, leaving her in a form-fitting black undersuit. It was similar to the clothing they all wore, of course, but Jesse had seen the gorgeous curves beneath, and the mix of sexy and badass she was rocking was a fucking appealing combination. Since Tara was Jud's standby diver, she slid a gray neoprene beanie onto her head, then stepped into her suit next, turning so Bobby could zip her in.

Jesse and Bobby kitted up after her, even though they'd be waiting upwards of an hour for Jud to return to the surface. Stepping into his dry suit ratcheted up Jesse's anticipation. As he closed Bobby's back zipper, the guy jutted his chin at Jud. "They're always like this. He should just ask her out already."

Competing reactions whipped through Jesse. One colored by the way he and Tara had met and the night they'd shared—full of a desire he had no real right to feel and that was inappropriate at any rate. And the other, irritation on Tara's behalf.

"If you don't think it's challenging being the only woman on this team, you'd be wrong again…"

The memory of Tara's words squashed Jesse's personal reactions dead in their tracks. This was the bullshit she was talking about and it made him feel protective. "I just see a diver doing her job."

"Yeah, man, of course," Bobby said, zipping him into his suit. "Hunter's wicked smart. Team's lucky to have her."

Well, he couldn't argue with that. Her experience, competence, and expertise were clear in everything he'd seen her do. And fuck if every one of those things didn't make him feel more of what he was supposed to be trying to ignore.

Want. Need. Connection.

Shaking off the unwanted thoughts, Jesse forced himself to focus. Their routines and processes here were all familiar to him, but every team had its idiosyncrasies and he wanted to be fully prepared when it was his time to get wet. He put in his earpiece in time to hear the team's comms come to life.

Suddenly, Boone's voice was in his ear. "Okay, divers, let's dive safe and conservative. Surface marker buoys have been deployed. Jud, you're clear to descend. Run time starts now at oh seven twenty-one."

Jud doublechecked the dive computer on his wrist and gave a thumbs-up. On a *whirr*, the diving stage descended, carrying both diver and survey equipment to the bottom. George ensured the smooth entry of the umbilical, which supplied their air from the surface. Tara was busy on a laptop, monitoring the output from Jud's dive computer and recording the data into his dive profile that logged every dive each of them made.

Curious about whether Jud was sending any observations back yet,

Jesse moved beside Tara. Their computers were pre-programmed with common messages, and just then one popped up.

Moderate visibility

Not surprising. Storms stirred sand and debris up from the bottom, choking off the light already limited during descent.

"He's at thirty feet," Tara said, laser focused on the details of Jud's dive. "Forty. Fifty. Okay, he's down at fifty-eight." She made a quick calculation using the dive tables, then typed out a message to Jud.

34 minutes before reqd deco

Jud's replies came in quick succession:

Roger

Survey underway

Admiring her work, Jesse nodded. Compared to the navy, commercial diving played it safe in determining the amount of time you could stay down before requiring decompression stops on the ascent. But then again, nothing was gained by taking risks or being aggressive. While diving posed some hazards, nothing here was life or death, unlike the navy.

And Jesse was fucking grateful for that. Because he'd had enough life-or-death for a lifetime. He wore those losses on his skin, where he'd inked one star for every fallen friend and teammate. Twenty-two in all—twenty KIAs and two suicides. So enough was e-fucking-nough.

Forty minutes later, Jud was back on the *GD*. Taking off his helmet, his first words were "You gotta love life in flippers!"

Jesse chuckled despite himself. They were complete opposites—Jud was blond and gregarious and good-humored if a little ridiculous, while Jesse was dark and reserved and moody, which he had to own. But he liked the guy a lot. And he could probably use more ridiculous in his life anyway.

Jud was all business after that, giving Jesse the rundown of what he'd accomplished and where Jesse needed to pick up. Game plan in place, Jesse was ready to go.

He checked his computer, gave a thumbs-up, and grasped the railing as the diving stage descended. Even with his thermals, the water was cold as a motherfuck, but it had him smiling behind his viewport.

He might've let down too many families for not being able to bring all his guys home and that might've made him bad for the EOD field. But *this?* This he could totally do.

* * * *

"Good first day?" Tara asked as they hosed down their dry suits late that afternoon.

Jesse smiled as he hung his suit to dry. "Great first day." It was true. He and Jud had finished more than a third of their zone, putting them a little ahead of schedule. And being back in the water had given Jesse an adrenaline high like he hadn't experienced in too damn long.

His satisfaction in that was about more than him just being an adrenaline junkie. Since he'd retired, one of the biggest challenges in transitioning to civilian life had been learning to live *without* threats and crises. After twenty years in some of the navy's most dangerous jobs, his brain was hardwired to operate under the expectation of the worst-case scenario coming true. Normal life sometimes felt like an illusion that would shatter at any moment because, for most of his life, the snafus had been his reality.

But in the water, he felt more centered. His brain and his body and his instincts felt more at ease, more like he was in his element.

"Feels good to get back in the water, doesn't it?" Jud asked, hanging his suit up next. "After I got out, being a landlubber about drove me nuts."

"Hell, yeah, it felt good," Jesse said. He waxed his suit's zipper, a key to maintaining its function.

Jud clapped him on the back. "Awesome to hear. See you in the mess. I'm fucking starving."

Jesse nodded, his belly aching with a hunger born of a good day's work. Exercise had always been one of the things that had kept him feeling balanced—or at least as balanced as he got—and he'd kept up his routine even after he retired. But there was nothing like ten hours of ocean swimming and battling the elements to exhaust you in all the best ways.

Well, except maybe sex, of course.

Like the thought had drawn her, Tara appeared at his side. Obviously his wishful thinking was alive and kicking.

She stretched onto tippy toes to hang her cleaned suit. "One of my best days ever was my first dive with CMDS. I never wanted out of the navy in the first place. Commercial diving gave me back the water at least."

"I got it," Jesse said, hanging it for her as his gut filled with surprise and curiosity. If she hadn't wanted out, had she been medically discharged? And if so, how had someone like him made it twenty years with only a few minor injuries, while people like her and the men he wore on his arm hadn't been so lucky? "I didn't want out so much as I thought it was best that I got out."

He could hardly believe he'd given voice to the thought, but she'd shared something important, so it made him feel like he could do the same.

She hugged her sweatshirt to her chest. "How long were you in?"

"I did my twenty."

Her eyebrows lifted as if he'd surprised her. "If you made it to retirement, I'd say you more than did your duty, Jesse. I knew a lot of EOD guys and more than a few burned out way before that."

When he'd found a pretty, funny girl at the bar last weekend, he'd never imagined that he'd also found someone with whom he could talk about things like this. "Yeah, well, I felt my fair share of that, too."

"I don't know how anyone could do that job and avoid feeling that way at least sometimes. Something that intense with so much always on the line and so many losses…."

He swallowed hard. "Yeah." It was all he could say in the face of such fundamental understanding. He'd never talked about feeling like he'd let his guys down. Not even once. Even though working in a relatively small community with such high casualty and suicide rates meant they literally lost someone every single week. And yet, it felt like Tara *knew*. He had to clear his throat.

For a long moment, they stood staring at each other, and that familiar sensation of the world closing in surrounded them. It was exactly how he'd felt before he kissed her that first time.

Suddenly, Tara hugged him.

Arms around him, her face on his chest, her embrace stole his breath. For just a second, it nearly knocked him on his ass. It was an utterly perfect moment, one even more meaningful than a kiss. Tara pulled back just as quickly, so fast that he'd barely been able to react.

"What was that for?" he asked, already missing the feel of her.

"Just looked like you needed it." A gust of wind had her rubbing her arms, and she peered around as if scanning to see if anyone saw them. "I'm gonna go get cleaned up. See you at dinner?"

He nodded and watched her walk away, gobsmacked because he *had* needed it. And somehow…*somehow* she'd known.

Chapter 9

Tara stumbled into her cabin feeling the good kind of tired. She'd enjoyed her first day back on the job and now she had a full belly. After getting so little sleep last night, she couldn't wait to climb into her berth.

The *GD* had five crew cabins—a captain's quarter for Boone and four small two-berth cabins for the rest of them. There were also cabins for visitors, like the scientific teams they sometimes worked with. When she'd joined the team, Boone had given her the choice to sleep where she was comfortable. Not wanting to be separated out from the team, she'd taken the open berth in Bobby's cabin—which lasted approximately two hours upon learning that he snored like a chainsaw, which was why he slept alone in the first place. That night, she'd moved to the unoccupied cabin, which had led to a great deal of hilarity the next morning at breakfast.

But on a night like tonight when she was so bone tired, Tara didn't mind sailing solo at all. Killing the overhead light, she fell into the bottom berth and tugged the curtain closed around her little bed. The rock and roll of the boat was comfortingly familiar. She got her pillow and her blankets and her position just right and let out a long sigh.

Her eyelids fell closed. And behind them she saw Jesse.

Tara groaned. "Not again, stupid brain."

Except what she saw wasn't exactly like last night. Not that she could *forget* the image of him going down on her. But after today, she had a whole host of new images of the man.

Of him in the form-fitting black thermals that outlined every muscle. There was just no help for the fact that some men in any kind of uniform or gear were just sexy—and Jesse was definitely one of them.

Of his utterly breathtaking smile when he ascended from the water after his first dive, clearly exhilarated.

Of the unspoken pain on his handsome face when he'd talked about feeling like it was best that he got out of the navy. She'd known so many people who internalized the guilt of other sailors getting injured or dying, and it made her chest hurt to think that Jesse might do that to himself.

And then there was the hug. Tara hadn't meant to do it. It'd been pure instinct. She'd pulled back so fast she hadn't even let him react. But behind that instinct had been her conscious mind yelling, *You were the one who said nothing should happen again!*

Right. She had. And she'd had good reason. But their first day on the job had proven that she could focus and work with him. So maybe he wasn't the problematic distraction she'd thought he would be?

No. Nope. *Don't even take the chance, Tara.*

She sighed in the darkness. *Fine.*

With that renewed determination in mind, Tara didn't cross the line at all the next day, and things were totally normal between them. No awkwardness over her unwise hugging at all. The team had come together like clockwork, even as the weather worsened and the seas got choppier. Jud and Jesse had accomplished their survey of another third of the zone, leaving them less than a third tomorrow. At that rate, they'd finish right on time.

By the end of the day, it felt like Jesse had been part of the team forever. The group's chemistry felt natural, easy, and it made Tara happy for him. At dinner, Jesse was telling stories and joking around like the rest of them. Chowing on Boone's famous beef stew, he said, "That sunken ship outside our zone? It's the *USS Arthur Radford*. Spruance-class destroyer. Longest ship ever reefed in the Atlantic. Over five hundred feet long. Imagine having served on that."

George nodded. "I had a buddy who did. I think it would feel weird as hell. May she rest in peace."

Jud pointed with his spoon. "Better that they sunk her on purpose than it being a wreck."

"It would be weird to have served on it, but at least it has a new purpose." Tara thought back to the reading she'd done when she'd spent a long weekend over here last October. "I think there are eight ships that've been sunk off the coast as part of an artificial reef program. There's even a sub—the *Blenny*, I think. And there are some wrecks around here, Jud, so beware the ghosts."

He smirked. "I ain't afraid o' no ghost." Groans and laughter followed.

"There's a German U-Boat south of here, too," Mike said.

"Shit, I didn't realize that," Jesse said. "Must be some killer recreational diving here then."

"There is," Tara said.

"Fantastic," Mike said at the same time. They laughed. "There's a two-hundred-foot World War I vessel in 80 feet of water that's one of my faves. Like a playground for divers."

"Too bad the weather isn't clear enough to stick around and take a peek at any of these," Jud said. "Tomorrow's going to be fun."

Boone shook his head. "If by 'fun' you mean 'challenging'…" One of the things Tara really liked about her boss was how concerned he always was for their safety, so she wasn't surprised that the worsening weather was weighing on him. "I've been thinking we should stay the weekend and finish on Monday."

Jud frowned. "You'll lose money if we do that. Jesse and I can handle it."

Nodding, Jesse said, "I'll defer to your call, of course, Boone. But I've worked in worse. I'm not concerned. And we're ahead of schedule so we might not need as long tomorrow."

"See?" Jud said, helping himself to seconds of stew. "We got this."

Tara's belly went on a little loop as she scooped the last bit of the rich soup from her own bowl. Not because she doubted her teammates, but because any heightened risk poked at her anxiety. But risk couldn't be entirely negated from diving. Even if seas were calm and visibility was perfect, there was always some danger. Equipment malfunctions, loss of diving weights, a suit blowup, stings, diver panic—not common but not unheard-of either. "Count me in," she said. Bobby agreed.

Boone got seconds, too. "I'll make the call at oh six hundred so I can let the AWE team know one way or the other. They're also keeping an eye on things."

That evening, a few of them stayed in the mess hall to play poker for a while. "You boys ready to part with your cash?" Tara asked, directing her teasing gaze first at Jud, then George, then Jesse.

"Oh, now, listen to this," George said.

"Do I need to be scared?" Jesse asked, grinning at her. She did a few tricks as she shuffled the cards, and his eyes widened. She raised an eyebrow at him.

Jud sat on his chair backwards. "Yes. Very. Fucking cleaned me out last time."

"Then why are we playing with her?" Jesse chuckled.

Holding out his hands in exasperation, Jud said, "Luck's gotta be my lady some time."

"Keep telling yourself that," Tara said to a round of laughter. "What do you gentlemen want to play?"

Jesse looked to the guys. "What is she worst at?"

George gave him a droll stare. "Nothing."

Jesse's gaze got more appreciative with each new revelation, and Tara was quite enjoying it. "It's true," she said, thanking her dad for the millionth time for teaching her how to play poker—and play it well. Her nerd's brain loved thinking through the statistics and odds of it all.

"Texas Hold 'em, then," Jesse said. As Tara started dealing, he arched a brow. "So you have an encyclopedic knowledge of sunken ships, you're a card shark, you worked SPECWAR, and you belong to a fight club?"

The reference to information she'd shared when they'd first met unleashed butterflies in her belly. "Yep."

"Wait, you belong to a fight club?" Jud's gaze cut up from his hole cards.

"It's not really about the fighting," she said. "But, yeah."

Jud scratched his chin. "How's a fight club not about fighting?"

Tara peeked at her cards, quite happy with her pocket kings. "It's called Warrior Fight Club. It's only open to veterans. They train us in MMA as a way to help people deal and adjust, post-service."

George tilted his head. "Like a kind of alternate therapy?"

Heat filtered through Tara's cheeks, even though it only took one look to know something bad had happened to her. "Yeah." She laid down the three cards of the flop—a king, a three, and a ten. Annnd now she had trip' kings. Excellent.

Sure enough, Jud glanced at her throat. "Huh. Sounds cool. Anyone can come?"

Tara looked at him. "Yeah. You interested?"

They did a round of betting, and George folded. "When does it meet?" Jud asked.

She dealt the turn card, the three of diamonds, which created a pair of threes in the community cards. Tara now had a freaking awesome hand—a full house, kings over threes. "Saturday afternoons. And then a bunch of us usually go out to dinner."

Jud bet aggressively, and Tara guessed he had the other king. The poor guy thought his two pairs were a winner. "Sure, I'm interested," he said. "What d'ya say, Jesse?"

It was Tara's turn to bet next, and she raised Jud's bet.

"Fuck." Jud glared at her. She just smiled.

Jesse shook his head. "I'm gonna let you two fight over that." He folded his cards. "Sure, I'll come check it out."

Tara's belly was back to doing loops again. She was actually excited to bring people she knew into the club, but it would mean even more time spent with Jesse. As it was, her body needed no convincing that she liked him, *wanted* him. Whether she should or not. "Great," she said, dealing the river card after Jud met her bet.

The three of hearts—putting trip' threes in the community cards.

Oh. *Oh*. In her head, she was yelling, *You don't want to do it, Jud!*

But then, of course, Jud did it. "I'm all in."

Tara's poker face was *good*, so she sat calmly as he pushed his whole stack of quarters into the pot. Then he smirked at her so hard that she lost all her sympathy for him.

"Wow," she said, grimacing down at her cards like she was really worried.

"No shame in bowing out gracefully," Jud said.

Which was when Tara called his bet. "Read 'em and weep, Mr. Taylor." She laid down her kings, revealing her full house, kings over threes.

Jud flew out of his chair. "Fuck. *Fuck*."

Chuckling, George flipped over Jud's cards for him. Just like she suspected, he had the same but weaker hand, threes full of kings.

The rest of the night continued pretty much the same way, with Tara winning about seventy-five percent of the hands she played through to the river card. She really, really liked Hold 'em.

George was the first to drop out of the game. Jud went next, having written an IOU on her forearm for $65. And then it was just her and Jesse, who was a smart if a little bit of a conservative player. But that approach meant he'd lost the least of the three men.

"Still game?" she asked, collecting the cards from the last hand.

"I enjoyed the hell out of watching you play, but you already took enough of my money. Thank you very much."

She laughed and made a chicken noise, and he threw his cards at her, making her laugh harder.

"Damn straight. Where the hell did you learn to play like that?" He leaned down to retrieve some of the spilled cards.

"My dad. He was also navy. We moved around a lot, of course, so he helped fill my spare time 'til I made friends by playing poker with me. I got good."

He smirked. "You don't say."

She smirked back. "After I graduated high school, I played some at the tournament level. Probably could've kept at that for a while, but I decided to join the navy instead." What she didn't tell him was how much she'd second-guessed her decision when, just six months after enlisting, her mom died unexpectedly of a heart attack. She'd hated thinking of her dad all alone, but he'd been nothing but supportive.

"I joined right out of high school, too," he said, his gaze more appraising. She'd guessed that about him when he'd revealed he served his full twenty. He didn't look old enough to have served twenty years as it was. So enlisting after graduation was something else they had in common then.

And damn, why did she like when he looked at her so much? She didn't just feel observed, she felt…*seen*. In a way she hadn't in so long.

Tara slipped the cards into their box and rose. "We gotta be up in six hours anyway." Jesse groaned, making her laugh. "It'll be a great navy day." It was something her dad said so often when she was a kid.

He rolled his eyes. "Roger that."

They walked aft, then descended a ladder to the cabin deck. Jesse reached his door first.

"Good night, Jesse." She kept moving because she didn't trust herself to remain close to him.

"Good night, Daddy Warbucks." He threw her a grin. A really sexy grin. One she wanted to kiss off his face. For starters.

Resisting that urge, Tara held up her bag of winnings. "It's good to be queen." And then she quickly closed herself in her room before she broke her own rules.

Chapter 10

Tara was soaked, and she wasn't one of the divers who'd been in the ocean. It had been pouring for hours. Only the fact that the wind remained moderate kept them from calling the whole thing off. Plus, the *GD* was big enough that it remained fairly stable despite the minor swells. Still, it was an exercise in balance for her and Bobby to do what they needed for the team's working divers.

Luckily, it wasn't as rough for Jud and Jesse on the bottom as it was for them on the surface, but that didn't mean it was perfect, either. The good news was that they only had one more dive to complete the survey of the remaining zone. Jesse was ascending now and Jud was ready to dive as soon as he hit the surface.

Tara and Bobby were huddled around the waterproof computer system when Bobby frowned. And then Tara saw Jesse's message that explained why.

Skip safety stop

"Shit," Bobby said. "It must be too rough for the diving stage."

As Bobby communicated that to Boone and Mike, Tara looked over the edge of the boat. A safety stop was a three-minute stop made about fifteen feet beneath the surface during the final part of the ascent. Considered a best practice for safe diving at any depth beneath twenty feet, it was mandatory for deeper dives or dives where they'd surpassed the maximum diving time limits. In those situations, a diver had to make controlled ascents with occasional stops to allow his body to adjust to changes in ambient pressure and off-gas nitrogen absorbed while diving.

The diving stage broke the water, and Jesse appeared calm. Unharmed. Fine. Of course, he was a professional who'd probably worked under more hazardous circumstances. But still.

When the stage was secure, he came aboard and he and Jud immediately exchanged information. "Visibility's declining," Jesse said. "But there's only two survey spots left."

"You okay, son?" Boone asked.

Jesse wiped at his face. "I'm good. But it's too rough at the surface to chance the safety stop."

Boone nodded. "Still want George to check you out."

"That's not necessary, sir."

Arching an eyebrow, Boone gave him a stern look. It wasn't one he wore often, which made it all the more impactful when he hit you with it. "Get checked."

"Roger that." Jesse clapped Jud on the back. "Your umbilical's gonna want to yank you around, so just watch it."

Jud gave him an okay gesture, and Tara attached his regulator to his helmet. And then he was on the diving stage and going down.

Tara had to stay focused on Jud's dive profile, but she couldn't help being curious as George led Jesse away. Staying down too long and ascending too aggressively could cause a diver all sorts of problems, not all of which manifested right away. The most common was the joint pain caused by nitrogen bubbles hitting your blood and tissues, known as "the bends" or decompression sickness. But injury from expanding air was also possible to the ears, sinuses, and lungs. And far more serious were arterial gas embolisms and nitrogen narcosis, which could impair brain function, giving an affected diver headaches and visual disturbances, impairing judgment, and even causing paralysis.

Jesse's fine, Tara told herself. And she made herself believe it so she could do her job.

"Jud's down at sixty-one feet," she called, calculating his max dive time on the tables. It hadn't even been an hour since he'd completed his last dive, which limited how long he could stay down this time.

19 minutes before reqd deco

Damn that was tight. Jud's replies came in quick succession:

Roger

Poor visibility

Survey underway

The rain turned to more of a drizzle, and Tara breathed a sigh of relief. They were almost done. Jesse and Jud had really kicked ass today.

When George and Jesse returned, Jesse was holding a mask to his face with one hand and carrying the portable oxygen cylinder from the resuscitator kit in his other.

George reported to Boone, but everyone gathered around. "Anderson's good. Recommending thirty minutes of oxygen as a precaution."

Boone clapped Jesse on the shoulder. "Decompression chamber if you need it, okay?"

Jesse nodded, but he didn't look too happy about any of it. Tara winked at him and gave him a little smile. In her experience, SPECWAR people made terrible patients, so she suspected it was probably hard for him to accept the help.

He rolled his eyes at her, but his expression beneath the mask shifted, eased.

As the rain backed off, the wind picked up—and so did the waves. Tara checked the dive time and sent an update to Jud:

Ten minutes to reqd deco

Rain decreased but wind gusts to 25 knots

She frowned when he didn't respond right away, but finally his message came through: *Roger*

Then four minutes later:

Survey complete

Returning to stage

"He's done," Tara said.

Mike sprang into action, preparing to reel up the diving stage. Boone returned to mission control to monitor the reports Jud's computer would be uploading.

Beam me up, Scotty

Tara grinned at the team joke they'd had programmed into all the dive computers. She motioned to Mike to bring Jud up.

She wasn't sure exactly what happened next. One minute, the winch was *whirring* as it lifted the diving stage. The next, the wind kicked up hard enough to drive a line of swells against the *GD*'s haul, rocking the girl's big ass to starboard. It shouldn't have been that remarkable, except that the winch motor made a grinding sound and then there was a high-pitched metallic rasp.

George and Mike flew to the mechanicals to see what'd happened, and Boone nearly skidded onto deck like he'd hauled ass the second things had gone fubar.

Tara's gut dropped as she typed out a query to Jud: *Report status*

No answer.

Jesse appeared at her side without his oxygen, his expression like a dark storm. "Something happened to one of the cables."

That was all she needed to hear. "Bobby!" Tara called, her brain going on autopilot.

The man was there in an instant, already knowing why she'd called him. She was Jud's standby diver. It was her responsibility to go to his assistance.

She checked her dive computer then grabbed her helmet. "Gonna use the scuba," she said, referencing the self-contained underwater breathing apparatus she'd wear harnessed to her back. It would give her an extra bail-out cylinder in case Jud's air had been compromised in the accident and more freedom of movement than an umbilical connected to surface-supplied air.

Bobby had her fully kitted in thirty seconds.

Tara turned for the deck's open edge, catching Jesse's concerned expression just before she performed a stride entry, maintaining a vertical posture until she was fully submerged.

Her hand found the shot line that connected the dive buoy to the dive site on the bottom, and even though she registered the cold temperature and the waves trying to pull her this way and that, her sole focus was on descending as quickly as possible, being careful to equalize her pressure to prevent barotrauma as she went deeper. Twenty feet. Thirty. Forty.

Diver 3 in the water

She peered upward but was already too deep to make Bobby out. It was good that he was coming, because he could handle assessing the equipment damage.

Fifty. Fifty-five. Darkness enveloped her. Her helmet light only penetrated a few feet in front of her. Tara touched bottom and oriented herself in the direction where the stage should be.

It only took her twenty seconds to locate the tall square structure—and then Jud himself.

He was calmly sitting on the bottom facing the metal box.

Tara made an okay symbol with her fingers, asking him with hand signals if he was injured.

Jud pointed to his foot.

Leaning down, Tara found that the stage had trapped one of Jud's feet beneath it when it hit the bottom. She dug at the sand, attempting to create a cavity beneath his foot that would free him. But the bottom was more compacted than she expected. They needed to move the stage.

Just then, Bobby arrived, and Tara signaled the problem to him.

Bobby gestured that he would lift the stage, allowing Tara to haul Jud out of the way.

She gave him an okay symbol and grabbed Jud under his arms from behind.

Hands under the stage bottom, Bobby strained until it finally gave enough that she could pull their teammate free.

She hooked a buddy line to Jud's suit and sent two pre-programmed messages:

Diver retrieved

Status good

With a thumbs-up, she told Bobby she was hauling Jud to the surface.

Jud's dive computer told her he'd missed his maximum dive time without decompression by six minutes, so she followed its guidance on the depth ceiling where he'd need to make his first deco stop.

Shot line in her hand, they ascended to forty-five feet. Tara made a gesture of her hand rising and falling over her chest, asking about his air. Jud gave her an okay, and then they ascended to his next ceiling. They stopped again at thirty feet. At fifteen feet, Tara made him pause for the final safety stop. Even though the water churned around them, she didn't want to risk him further injury.

Finally, they broke the surface. Waves drove them toward the ladder, and hands helped pull Jud onboard. And then her.

As soon as their helmets were off, Jud recounted what'd happened. "The stage was probably about twenty feet off the bottom when the whole thing jolted and swung to probably forty-five degrees. Dumped my ass to the bottom and then fuck if the stage didn't come down right on top of me. I almost got out from underneath it." Tara unzipped him, and the others helped him out of his dry suit as he spoke. "Landed on my foot."

"Let's take a look," George said, the medic kit at the ready.

Since Bobby was still in the water, she didn't shed her scuba gear. Just in case. She joined Jesse at the dive computer, where he was standing watch over the other man's dive.

His gaze cut to hers, and his eyes were dark fire. "You okay?"

"Fine," she said. The answer was a hundred per cent rote. Because Tara was completely and utterly numb. "What's going on with Bobby?"

He tilted the screen toward her, and she read the incoming messages.

Stage cable 2 snapped

Repairing

Standby

Before she and Jud had ascended, Tara had seen one of their welding kits resting by the shot line. Welding broken cable wasn't a long-term solution by any means, but it would hopefully be enough for them to get the stage back onboard the *GD*.

"Ask him if he needs help," Tara said, the wind blowing tendrils of hair in her face.

Jesse's eyebrows slashed downward. "It's too soon for you to go back in."

"Not if he needs help it isn't."

Scowling, Jesse sent the query.

Repair complete

Even though that was good news, Tara frowned. Restlessness stalked her blood.

The computer dinged another incoming message: *Beam me up, Scotty*

This time, the silly message didn't make her smile.

It only took another fifteen minutes before the crisis was completely resolved. Bobby ascended and the team worked to get the stage secured on the deck. They were going to have to rethread a new cable, but that would be a job for a different day.

"Told you today would be fun," Jud said where he still sat on the deck. Under a bag of ice, the top of his foot was already turning purple. His humor was met with a low murmur of chuckles and smart-ass comebacks.

And then everything was back to their normal routine. Securing equipment. Cleaning suits. The only thing that stood between them and dry land was one last video briefing with the crew from AWE, and Boone, Jesse, and Jud were the only ones required to be in on that.

"I'll take care of your suit," she told Jud. "You take care of you."

George helped their teammate to his feet, and then gave him a pair of crutches to use until they could x-ray his foot. Jud used them to come right to her. "Thank you."

His unusual seriousness pricked at the backs of her eyes. But no way was she letting tears come in front of him—or any of them. "No big deal."

He narrowed those dark blue eyes at her. "Big fucking deal, Tara. So thank you."

"You're welcome," she managed. Then she nodded her head at the closest hatch. "Go get off your feet."

"Yes, ma'am."

Boone was the next to poke at the emotions she didn't want to face. "You did good, Tara. Real good."

She nodded, her throat suddenly too tight to speak.

Heading back inside, Boone pointed at Jesse. "We're on with AWE in fifteen."

"Roger that," he said. And then his gaze was back on her.

But Tara kept her eyes on her work. Hosing down Jud's suit. Then her own. Hanging them up. Waxing their zippers. She performed each new task almost mechanically, but she gave them all her focus. Because she'd rather focus on them than the other things she was going to have to confront sooner or later.

Finally, she moved to the computer to complete Jud's dive profile and enter one for herself.

Jesse appeared at her side. "How are you doing?" His voice was low, serious, concerned.

"Don't," she said. Because she couldn't answer him. Not yet.

He squeezed her shoulder. "I'm here, Tara."

A quick nod. Then he was gone. Which was one less distraction keeping her from facing the tsunami of emotions cresting inside her.

Chapter 11

Approaching the Ocean City inlet meant it would be only fifteen minutes until they'd be docked. And Jesse hadn't seen Tara once since he'd left her on the deck of the *GD*.

"Don't."

That one word wouldn't stop echoing in his head. Because it was just…off. Wrong. Nothing like the Tara he'd come to know. Ever since that exchange, intuition had unleashed prickles up and down his spine. His gut told him she wasn't okay.

Not physically harmed, no. But not all injuries were visible. He knew that as well as anyone.

The problem was, he couldn't think of a good explanation for going to check on her, not when they'd played it that they'd been strangers that first day. He didn't think she'd appreciate him acting in any way that might reveal anything about their real relationship…

Whatever the hell it actually was, Jesse didn't know. He just knew that watching her jump into the roiling ocean to dive to an accident site in sixty-foot waters had been damn hard to do. Not because he didn't think she could handle it. Not because she wasn't competent. Not because she wasn't capable of rescue and recovery. But because she meant *more* to him than just a colleague.

How much more, he didn't know.

Bullshit, a little voice in his head said.

Fine. More than a friend, even.

It was almost more than he could believe—that he'd developed such a strong connection when he'd always half wondered if there was something wrong with himself on that score. He hadn't been close with his dad, and as he'd disappointed his father more and more during high school, it'd impacted his relationship with his mother and his sister, Willa. As a result, he barely knew his nine-year-old nephew, Alex.

As an adult, he'd had plenty of friendships but only a handful of relationships that'd been serious or long enough to elevate to the status of girlfriend.

Yet, here he was, fighting the magnetic pull that apparently every cell in his body felt to go check on Tara. Take her in his arms and make them both feel better. And then figure out how to convince her that they had to give *more* a shot.

But he didn't do any of that.

Just as they motored into the marina, Tara appeared on deck. Showered. Dressed. Hair in a loose braid. She chatted with George, checked on Jud, and generally acted normal. But Jesse's gut wasn't buying it. Her normally animated face appeared almost a mask of expected expressions. Her tone wasn't quite right. Her eyes were flat, almost distant. How he could read her so well so fast he wasn't sure, but Jesse didn't think he was wrong.

They got the *Going Deep* moored and then Boone gathered them on the deck, making it easier to include Jud, who could only navigate the ladder to the bridge with some difficulty. The sea had taken a bite out of the guy today, but he was still sitting there laughing and joking around about how his foot had turned into an eggplant emoji, *har har*. He'd made every single one of his teammates laugh over it, clearly proving his expertise at using humor to defuse a stressful situation.

Jesse had to respect that.

Boone stood with his hands on his hips, the day's crisis still clearly weighing on the man's shoulders. "Listen, gang, after today, I think you all deserve a bit of a respite. So unless there are any objections, I'd like to treat everyone to dinner and put y'all up in the Holiday Inn for the night. We can leave at first light, but I think that would be better than trying to get home after the day we had."

Appreciative words rose up from the group.

Boone cleared his throat. "I want to apologize for not playing today more conservatively—"

"Boone, no," Jud interrupted. "I was advocating for pushing forward today more than anyone. And besides that, it could've been that cable's time to go even if the weather had been fine."

"Agreed," Jesse said. The others all felt the same, including Tara, who…Jesse did a doubletake. Because she was hugging herself so hard that her knuckles had gone white.

Boone nodded, his expression moved by the support. "I appreciate that. But all of you…you're my team. It's my job to take care of you. I hate to see any of you hurt, especially on the job—and especially when I'm in charge. I want you to know it won't happen again."

While everyone reassured Boone, Jesse stood there a little gobsmacked.

Because, man, did his boss's words hit him right in the chest—right in the *memories*, if he were honest. Because as *Chief Anderson*, he'd had to give similar talks more than once. A leader was always accountable for what happened to those under his command, which was why he'd felt the weight of every EOD tech he'd lost. During his last deployment in Iraq, his team had performed one hundred EOD missions, including forty improvised explosive devices, twenty-one unexploded ordnance calls, eighteen suspect improvised explosive devices, twelve post-blast assessments, and nine suspect vehicle improvised explosive devices. That was just *one* of his many deployments.

But the number Jesse most remembered…the one that felt most important…. That number remained twenty-two.

Before long, they'd packed up and made for the same restaurant they'd visited at the start of the project. Jud had made the case for eating before they ran him to the ER to get his foot scanned, so the whole team was together as they celebrated having emerged from a crisis relatively unscathed and having finished the lucrative surveying project on schedule.

While Jesse enjoyed himself, he couldn't stop sneaking glances at Tara. She laughed when she was supposed to laugh, answered questions when someone posed one to her, and seemed engaged in the banter. But she mostly pushed the food around on her plate. And when she'd reached for her drink, Jesse had caught the unmistakable glimpse of fingernail marks in the palm of her hand.

Knowing she was hurting—and putting on a show to appear otherwise—was eating Jesse up inside. Especially because the day had left him almost exhilarated, as if the part of his brain set to expect bad things to happen could be quiet for once in the wake of an actual snafu. That was probably twisted, but it didn't make it any less true.

Finally, they were back in the elevator at the Holiday Inn, minus

Boone, George, and Jud, who'd all gone to the hospital. Mike and Bobby got off on the second floor, leaving Jesse and Tara alone.

"Funny meeting you here," Jesse said, trying to reach her with humor. Even though what he wanted to say was *Please tell me what's wrong. Please let me help. Please lean on me.*

She gave him a little smile even as she rolled her eyes at him. "Are we neighbors again? I'm in 420."

His gut fell, which was damn telling. "Nope. I'm in 302. This is me," he said as the bell dinged for the third floor. "G'night."

"Night," she said, those pretty blue eyes too damn flat.

The door closed, and Jesse caught it at the last minute, forcing it to ease open again. "Tara—"

She shook her head, and now those eyes looked almost…scared.

He swallowed hard. "I'm in 302. Understand?"

"Yeah. 'Night," she said again, her voice no more than a whisper.

A rock in his gut, Jesse nodded and removed his hand. And hoped against hope that she'd come to him.

* * * *

By the time Tara got to her room, her hand shook so bad she had a hard time sliding the key card into her door.

"Come on," she said. "Come *on*."

Finally, she was in. She flicked on a light. Dropped her bag. And then paced because she didn't know what else to do with the overwhelming emotion inside her—the emotion from being involved in the first diving accident since her own.

Why was she freaking out so bad when she wasn't even the one who'd needed rescue? Instead, she'd been in the exact opposite role this time. And she'd been able to do her job without a single problem.

Except none of that seemed to matter to her brain which, as soon as she'd known Bobby was safe, had started offering up flashbacks of what'd happened to her. And it didn't seem to matter to her central nervous system which, now that no one was watching, had her body shaking uncontrollably. And it didn't seem to matter to her instincts, which told her that she should be terrified—as terrified as the day she'd nearly died in the ocean several years before.

Even though there wasn't a single damn thing to be scared of.

But Tara couldn't seem to logic herself out of this one.

She'd tried. Over and over again. On the *GD*, she'd retreated to her cabin, used the breathing techniques she'd learned in counseling, and had attempted to immerse herself in her environment by focusing on things she could see and smell and hear. But none of it worked.

And now...in the middle of her hotel room, she burst into tears. Went down to her knees. Curled into a ball and just...sobbed.

I can't let them see me like this. I can't let them see me like this. They can never see me like this.

That was what her anxiety was worried about. That if her teammates ever knew she was this fragile, they'd never again trust her to have their backs. They'd see a weak link instead of an equally qualified teammate. Boone would second-guess hiring her in the first place.

A small, distant-sounding part of her mind tried to remind her that anxiety lied, but she couldn't believe it. Not now. Not when doing her job had left her so shattered.

Oh, God, they can't see.

Fearing that someone would hear her, she tugged at the corner of the bedspread and pulled part of it down so she could bury her face in it. And then she let herself scream—scream in a way she hadn't been able to do when that cable had sliced open her throat under thirty feet of water.

If she'd been as deep then as Jud was earlier, she wouldn't be alive today.

And now she realized that in a part of her brain she hadn't let herself recognize in the moment, she'd feared finding Jud dead at the bottom of the Atlantic. Part of her had been terrified that she wouldn't get to Jud as fast as her team had gotten to her—and then it would be her fault that he'd died, the same way that it had been due to her team's speed, skill, and care that she'd been saved.

The tears came harder. So hard that her stomach hurt and her face ached and her throat felt raw. So hard that it was difficult to breathe.

Come on, Tara. Five things you can see.

"T-the blanket," she whispered. "M-my hands. The c-carpet." She pressed a hand to her mouth as more tears came. "T-the light," she rasped. "My knees."

She attempted a deep breath, but shuddered too hard to manage it.

Four things you can hear.

"M-me," she said. "T-the heater." But there was nothing else. She couldn't get to four. The room was too quiet. Her pain was too loud.

Skip it! Three things you can feel.

Through her tears, she managed to say, "C-carpet is rough. Everything…" She swallowed hard. "Everything hurts. Everything hurts so much." The admission brought more tears.

Come on, what's your third?

The problem was, she couldn't feel anything else right now. But then, unexpectedly, her memory offered up something she'd felt in the past. Something that'd felt *good*: her face resting against Jesse's chest. When she'd thought he'd been hurting and she'd wanted to make it better. Even if just a little.

"Jesse," she whispered.

Why was she thinking about him right now? When he wasn't even here, in her environment? That wasn't how this exercise worked.

"I'm in 302. Understand?"

He knew. Despite her best efforts to lock her reactions down, he knew.

Besides that, he is *here and you know it. And not just in room 302.* She snuffled into the blanket as the thought caught her off guard. What did that even mean?

Thinking of him was the first time since she'd given in to the panic attack that she'd felt something different—something comforting….

Affection.

She liked Jesse. Not just as a teammate. Not just as a friend. Beyond that, who the heck even knew? But she saw those concerned eyes in her mind and she heard his voice in her ear and she felt his chest under her face.

He *was* here. Inside her.

Tara closed her eyes and tried to hold on to *that* feeling. And wondered if she should take him up on his offer.

But the fact was, they *were* teammates. He couldn't see her like this any more than any of the rest of them could. And besides, she needed to get herself out of this emotional hole. She had to convince *herself* that she could pull it together, even when she lost it so bad.

Tara needed to do this on her own.

So she forced herself to think of two things she could smell.

Except the carpet cleaner was the only thing strong enough to penetrate the congestion her crying had caused. But she was counting that as a victory.

Which left one thing she could taste.

And somehow it felt appropriate that her answer was snot. Because yay her.

The tears hadn't ended. But the sobs had.

The pain hadn't gone away. But she could breathe again.

Her body aches were still there. But she wasn't shaking anymore.

It was working. Tara was doing it.

"You're okay," she whispered. "And Jud's okay."

She blew out a long breath and forced herself into a sitting position.

"That's true," she said to the empty room. And she'd had a hand in both of those things, hadn't she?

Coming out of the panic attack was huge progress, but the whole day had left her exhausted out of her mind. She washed her face. Pulled off her sweaty clothes and left them in a heap. Crawled into bed—without even bothering to turn off the lights.

She was almost asleep when she heard it.

Music coming from by her door.

Iconic music. One of her favorite songs of all time. One that was immediately identifiable with just the first four words: *You must remember this...*

Jesse. Jesse was playing *As Time Goes By* for her. It had to be him.

The echo of pain in her chest gave way to something else, something warm and full and new. She slid out of bed, remembered that she only wore underwear, and wrapped the blanket around her body like a cape.

A cell phone lay on the floor just inside her room.

Oh, Jesse.

Tara picked it up, took a deep breath, and opened her door.

Empty. The hallway was empty. From down the hall, she just made out the sound of the elevator doors closing.

For several long minutes, she stood there debating. Long enough that the short song ended...and then began again. She peered down at the screen to see that he'd set the song to repeat.

What a sweet, sweet man. This gesture...it was perfect. Perfect for her. And that...that was enough for now.

She closed her door. Crawled back into bed. Held Jesse's phone tight to her chest. And fell asleep to "Sam" singing her one of the most romantic songs she'd ever heard over and over and over again.

Chapter 12

Jesse spent all night debating what he'd done, especially when Tara didn't come after him. He hadn't played the song for her to make her respond. He'd done it because, having given in to the urge to go to her, he'd heard her sobbing.

Hand raised to knock, he'd frozen at her door. If it'd been him, he wouldn't have wanted anyone to witness it. And in case she felt the same way, he decided not to bother her.

Even though her anguish nearly broke his fucking heart.

But he'd been so worried for her that he'd sat outside her door just in case...well, he wasn't sure what he was exactly afraid of, but his gut told him she shouldn't be alone—even if she didn't know he was there.

After a long while, her cries had quieted. Little noises echoed from inside her room. He wasn't sure what made him think of the song, but once it was in his head, it felt like the best way to let her know she was going to be okay. And that he was willing to help.

But she hadn't come after him. And, after six hours of cruising back to DC, she still hadn't said anything to him beyond basic, polite necessities. She looked better today—her eyes were bright again and her expressions were genuine. And Jesse really hoped that meant he'd helped. Even if just a little.

They pulled into their home marina a little before one in the afternoon. Secured the *GD* and helped Boone stow equipment. Said what were apparently expected hellos to Mama D, who hugged every one of them as if they'd been off to war. Jesse thought it was sweet.

"Hey, Tara?" Jud called when they were all out in the parking lot. "Sorry about your fight club." He gestured to his bum foot.

"You can come any time, Jud." She crossed to where he stood, crutches under both arms. Miraculously, the crush injury to his foot hadn't broken any bones, so he'd be back to normal within a week or two. "Consider it a standing offer."

"Good deal," he said. "See ya Monday."

"Yep, sure will." She gave him a wave as he turned toward George's car, and then she crossed to her own car, parked right next to Jesse's. She opened her door. For a moment, Jesse thought she wasn't going to say a word, but then she looked over her shoulder at where he waited by his door. "Guess I should return this." She pulled his phone out of her back pocket and handed it across the roof to him.

Unsure how to read her, Jesse just nodded.

"So, you in?" she asked.

He frowned. "For what?"

"Warrior Fight Club?" She tilted her head, and the sun played off the golden highlights in her brown hair.

Her beauty fucking sucker-punched him. Just laid him right out.

"Yeah," he said, not needing to think about it. "I'm in."

"Good. We have just enough time to grab workout clothes from our places. Want to meet at the gym or, uh, I can pick you up?"

He nodded. "See you outside the Marriott in twenty?"

"Done," she said. And then she was in her car and backing out.

Okay, so…

That seemed like he hadn't fucked up by letting her know he'd been there last night.

He scratched his jaw. What else it told him, he didn't know. But he wasn't second-guessing it, either.

Which was why he was down on the street changed into workout gear and waiting within eighteen minutes.

Tara pulled up a minute later.

He got in. She took off. Neither of them said a word.

But the car was fucking *filled* with silent conversation. He didn't think he was imagining that.

Tara was the one who spoke first. "So, in case you're wondering how WFC works…" She glanced at him, and he nodded. "We meet once a week at Full Contact, a gym over in the U Street neighborhood. We start with yoga, which is good for getting your head on straight when…" She swallowed hard. "You know, when you need help with that. And, um, then we often pair off and do various kinds of training drills. Did you box or anything in the navy?"

"Yeah," he said. He had experience with more than boxing, but he didn't want to do anything to keep her from talking, now that she was finally doing it.

"Good. That's good. So we do training drills. We often do tag-team wrestling drills. And then we take turns pairing off to spar in the rings. That's about it, I think. Oh, Coach Mack is going to have some paperwork for you to complete before you can join in. Just usual stuff. And the gym has gear you can borrow."

Jesse nodded again. "Sounds good."

"It is. It's a good place. And awesome people from across all the branches. I'll make sure to introduce you to Sean Riddick—he was also navy. Oh, and Noah Cortez was EOD in the marines. So you'll fit right in. I bet you'll like WFC." Her chattiness now almost felt like she needed to fill the silence they'd had between them before. But he wasn't complaining. It was better than her not talking to him at all.

"Don't."

Worlds better.

"Bet I will," he said, letting himself do what he'd been wanting to do all morning. Get a good, long look at her pretty face. Her nose tilted up at the tip just a little, and her dark lashes were long. High cheekbones were tinged with a healthy pink, alive and vital.

Exactly how she made him fucking feel.

Tara caught him looking, but he didn't turn away. "What?"

"Nothing," he said, undeterred.

"Then why are you looking at me like that?"

Like I want you? Because I do. But he didn't say that. "Like what?"

"Um, I don't know. All…intense and stuff."

That eked a smile out of him. "All intense and stuff?"

"Yeah. You know."

He shook his head. "I really don't." He totally did.

She stopped behind a line of traffic at a red light. "You do, too. The whole tall, dark, and intense thing."

Jesse grinned. "Tall, dark, and intense?"

Her expression went totally exasperated, and she rolled her eyes. "Stop answering a question with a question."

"Why?" He was thoroughly enjoying himself now.

She glared at him. "Smart ass."

"I'll take that as a compliment."

"I didn't mean it as one."

"Hmm. How should I take 'tall, dark, and intense' then?" he asked, attempting to paint an innocent expression on his face.

Her cheeks went pinker. "I don't know!"

"I'm going with another compliment, I think."

"Oh, for crap's sake," she muttered under her breath.

"Regretting bringing me yet?" he asked.

Tara sighed. "I haven't decided." But there was no heat behind the words. "So are you going to answer the question?"

Jesse blinked. "Er, what was the question again?"

She rolled her eyes at him so hard. "Why you were looking at me."

Images flashed through his mind's eye. Of Tara, pinned against the wall in his hotel room. Of her sprawled out on his bed as he crawled over her. Of those blue eyes flashing up at him as she took him in her mouth. "Truth?"

"Always."

"Because I like looking at you." A fucking understatement given the way their teasing was stirring heat through his blood.

Deep pink roared over her face and down her throat. She swallowed audibly. "Oh."

"Mmhmm. Any other questions?" he asked.

"Um. No." She braked at an open parking space. "Anyway, we're here so prepare for me to kick your ass."

Jesse blinked. And then erupted with a deep belly laugh.

She glared as she parallel parked, killed the engine, and turned to him. "Think that's funny, huh?"

He tried to get himself under control, but when had he last so enjoyed himself? "Only because, if you did, it would be my favorite ass-kicking ever."

Tara narrowed her eyes at him. "You're still making fun of me."

He held up his hands. "No, ma'am. I'm telling you the God's honest truth. Always. Remember?"

Her expression was full of skepticism, and it was fucking cute. It really was. "You *want* me to kick your ass?"

Jesse turned toward her and leaned in. "No, Tara, but I sure as hell would enjoy you trying."

Her eyes went wide and she licked her lips. And, Jesus, her gaze dropped to his mouth. It took everything he had not to act on the need both of them clearly felt. But for now, he took great satisfaction in knowing he wasn't alone in feeling it. "Oh," she whispered.

"Yeah."

"So, um, we should, uh, go in. Now."

He nodded. "You lead, I'll follow."

"Right," she said, a sexy breathiness to her voice. She got out, retrieved her gym bag from the back seat, and came around to join him on the sidewalk that ran along the side of a big yellow-brick building—Full Contact MMA Training Center. They walked in silence all the way to the lobby, where a shiny steel reception counter filled one whole wall. She signed him in as a guest, and then they went down a flight of steps to a large rectangular gym space, open on one side, and housing two eight-sided cages on the other. "Let me introduce you to Coach Mack, and then I gotta go change."

There were about a dozen people already there, and he and Tara had barely started across the gym before the other club members started calling out greetings to her. A woman with long black hair pulled back in a sleek ponytail jogged over.

"Hey, Tara. I'm glad you made it back in time."

"Hey. Yeah, me too. It was close though; we came directly from work." She gestured to Jesse. "Dani, this is one of my co-workers, Jesse Anderson. He's prior navy EOD. Jesse, this is Daniela England. She was an army nurse and works at University Hospital now. And she's an all-around badass."

"I should have you do all my introductions," Daniela joked, extending her hand. "Hey, Jesse. Welcome."

"Hi, Daniela. Thanks."

"I'll see you out on the floor in a minute," Tara said to the other woman. "I'm gonna introduce Jesse to Coach." Dani gave them a wave, but they didn't quite make it to the benches before one of the men came to give Tara a hug.

"Hi, Tara. Dani said you might not make it," the man said. Tall with dark hair, the guy had some scars on the side of his face close to his ear.

She smiled at him, and it was clear just in these first few interactions what good friends everyone was. "Hi. Made it by the skin of my teeth. Noah, this is Jesse Anderson. We work together. Jesse, Noah's the marine EOD I was telling you about."

"Noah, how are you?" Jesse asked, shaking the man's hand. And damn if him being EOD didn't give his scars a whole new meaning.

"Good. Welcome, Jesse. You were EOD, too?"

"Yeah. Navy, though. But we worked with you guys often enough."

Noah nodded. "Yeah, we did. Good to have you, man. If you need anything or have any questions, don't hesitate to ask. Tara and I are the relative newbies in the bunch, but we've been here long enough to help you find your way around."

"Appreciate that," Jesse said.

Finally, they made it to where three men were congregated close to the benches. The oldest of them held a clipboard and was giving out assignments to the other two.

"Coach Mack?" Tara asked when there was a pause in the men's conversation. The coach was maybe ten years older than Jesse and wore full tattoo sleeves down both arms. "Jesse's a friend of mine and potentially interested in joining."

The man turned to him. "Welcome, Jesse. I'm John McPherson, but everyone calls me Mack."

Tara excused herself as Jesse returned the man's shake. "Glad to be here."

"Let me introduce you to our assistant coaches." Coach Mack waved the other two men closer. "Jesse, this is Leo Hawkins and Colby Richmond. You need anything, feel free to ask any of us." Leo had longish blond hair and solid black bands of ink around both biceps, and Colby had light brown skin and eyes, with close-cropped black hair.

"Will do," Jesse said, digging how welcoming everyone was. He wasn't even a part of this yet, but he already got the sense that this was more than a club. It felt more like a community. Given how distant he'd become with his mom and sister, Willa, that had always been one of his favorite things about the military, and it seemed they had it here, too.

Coach Mack glanced at his watch. "Hawk, Colby, why don't you handle warm-ups while I get Jesse squared away?"

As the men agreed, Jesse scanned the room to see that more people had arrived. Most were out on the blue mats stretching and shooting the shit, and there were maybe eighteen in all—and Dani and Tara were the only women.

Not interesting, my ass.

He and Coach sat on a bench. "So Jesse, tell me a little about yourself."

"Well, I retired from navy EOD last year and just moved to DC for a new job a few weeks ago."

Coach made some notes. "Any prior MMA experience?"

Jesse nodded. "I have a third-degree black belt in taekwondo. And I've done some boxing, wrestling, and judo."

"That's perfect," Coach said. "How about injuries?"

He shook his head. "I'm in good health."

"Prior injuries?"

Just then, Tara emerged from the locker room wearing a pair of gray spandex bike shorts, a loose-fitting tank over a sports bra, and a pair of black fingerless gloves. God, she had curves for days and drew him like a fucking magnet.

Jesse cleared his throat. "Oh, uh. Yeah. A few. Two GSWs, one to the thigh, the other to the shoulder. A mild TBI about eight years ago. And, you know, a million close calls." Like the time ten pounds of explosive had detonated a few feet behind him, tossing him a dozen feet in the air and burning and bloodying the backs of his legs. But it hadn't been his time, and he'd walked away from that roadside bomb—flipping his middle finger at the unseen insurgent who'd triggered it for good measure. Due to the nature of the gig, EOD techs suffered some of the most severe and life-changing injuries in the military. By comparison, Jesse had gotten off easy, so the attention on this wasn't entirely comfortable.

The older man listened intently, the kind of listening that made you feel heard. Understood, even. Finally, Coach Mack nodded and handed him some paperwork. "If you decide to join, get this back to me next time. You're clear to participate in everything except sparring today. Need your doc to sign off before that."

Nodding, Jesse tucked the packet into his duffle. "Thanks, Coach."

Clapping him on the back, Mack smiled. "Welcome to Warrior Fight Club."

Chapter 13

Jesse was liking WFC. The people were cool. It was the perfect way to keep up his exercise routine. And, just like at work, it was good to be around military personnel again—people who understood a lot about you and your experiences without even having to ask.

It also meant more time with Tara—even if sometimes Jesse was competing *against* her, like he was now.

They were on opposing sides of a tag-team grappling drill that focused on groundwork skills, which were all about achieving the submission of your opponent after a takedown. It shifted the focus of the fight from striking and kicking to wrestling and grappling. A good fighter needed to be competent at both, because in a true fight you had to be able to transition between different martial arts techniques sometimes in the space of just a few seconds.

Jesse had been placed on a team with Noah, Dani, and Leo, along with a few other people he'd only been able to talk to long enough to shake hands and exchange names.

"We're practicing groundwork here," Coach Mack said. "Your turn ends when you tap out or if you can get close enough to the edge to tag in one of your teammates. No striking, this is all about grappling for submission. Mo, Sean, you're up first."

Good-natured laughter and ribbing rumbled around the group, and then Jesse saw why. Both men were stacked. "Come on, Mo," Jesse said, cheering on his teammate.

With their teams forming a circle around them, the two men knelt facing one another. Both looked like mountains compared to the rest of the men in the room—none of whom were small. Jesse was half glad he wasn't starting off facing one of them. Mack gave the signal, and they tapped gloves. And then it was on—the grappling and the shit-talking.

"Hate to take you down, Mo," Sean said.

Mo actually managed to chuckle as they struggled for dominance. "Don't worry, I won't let you."

"Come on, Mo, get him," Dani said. "Teach that bigmouth a lesson."

"Love you, too, D," Sean called out.

It was teasing he paid for, though, because Mo managed to get a hold around Sean's chest and flipped him over, going for a rear-naked choke with a body lock. Sean just escaped it, rolling his hips in a way that weakened Mo's hold. Going for another lock, Mo rolled him, coming close enough to tag Dani in.

"Excellent," she said, rubbing her hands together.

Everyone congratulated Mo as he came out.

"Go get him, Dani," Noah said, humor plain in his voice.

Sean beckoned her closer. "Think you got what it takes, sweetheart?"

Dani's words were nearly a growl. "Don't fucking call me sweetheart."

Jesse felt like there was an insider joke he didn't yet know about these two, but as he watched Sean and Dani grapple, one thing was clear: tension *roared* off the two of them—and not all of it was about the fight. He couldn't help but wonder if they used to date or something, because there was a kind of volatile personal—maybe even sexual—chemistry between them.

Sean had bulk, but Dani had speed and flexibility. So even though Sean managed to pin her fairly quickly, she worked her way out of it just as fast and even managed to get her legs around his neck, pulling him onto his side. In a move that was all muscle, Sean flipped himself and pinned her again, but Dani was fighting it enough that he couldn't force her to tag out, so he managed to reach out a hand to tap a new teammate in—Tara.

It was the first time Jesse got to see just how good she was. She was stronger than Dani, though not as flexible, so the women were well-matched.

"Go, Dani," Jesse called, cheering for his teammate even though it killed him a little to do so. Dani came down on top of Tara, and Jesse thought the woman had her, but at the last minute, Tara twisted her hips and got a leg up and around the back of Dani's neck. Dani rolled out of the failed hold and reached out a hand…to him.

Jesse tagged in, and now it was him and Tara alone on the mats. And, damn, whether he pinned her or she pinned him, he'd be a fucking winner. "Is this when the ass-kicking happens, Hunter?"

She glared, then sprang for him.

Satisfaction and competitiveness roared through his gut, and nearly twenty years of training and experience held him in good stead as Jesse grabbed hold of Tara with his arms and worked to gain leverage with his legs. She successfully fought against getting pinned, though, and attempted to flip him. From the edge of the mats, their teammates called out guidance and encouragement, but all Jesse knew was the feeling of Tara's body against his.

She escaped him a second time, her moves full of pure grit, and he got the distinct feeling she was fueled by whatever she'd gone through the evening before.

That's right, baby. Take it out on me, he thought, coming up over her back and going for a rear-naked choke. He got a good handhold, and then flipped her until she was on top of him, her back to his chest. He got his heels around her thighs next and locked her to him, tight.

Tara struggled against the hold, trying to twist her hips and arch her back, but Jesse just squeezed harder, his body fucking singing from the contact. "Fuck," she rasped, tapping out.

He let go of her right away. "Good match," he said. She rolled her eyes at him but bumped his fist, and that was all the respite he had before another man he didn't know was in the ring with him and it was on again.

After just a few more minutes, Jesse managed to tag himself out. And as he watched Noah grapple with a guy who had some serious burn scars on his neck and shoulder, adrenaline pounded through his body. It was a rush, and Jesse wanted more of it. Which was the moment he decided he was going to join WFC.

The only part of the afternoon he didn't like was having to remain a spectator for all of the sparring, but he understood the rationale and would get his doctor appointment scheduled so he could be all in next time. When the whole thing wrapped up, Jesse let Coach know he'd be back, and then he joined Tara and about six others to hear them talking about going to dinner after everyone had cleaned up.

"So, what did you think?" she asked.

He peered down at her. Her face was ruddy and her hair was a shade darker from sweat. He'd found yet something else they shared in common in what was turning out to be quite a long list. And all of it made her appeal to him like no one had in so fucking long. Maybe ever. "As long as you're okay with it, count me in. I'd like to join."

Tara's smile was genuine. "I'm glad. I wouldn't have brought you if I minded. Game to join a small group of us for dinner?"

He was game to do anything if it meant hanging out with her. "Yeah, sounds good. I'm starving."

"Me, too," she said. "I can't promise Murphy's-level nachos, but this grill place we sometimes go to is really good."

Her referencing their first night together did nothing to diminish the high buzzing through his veins. "As long as they have food that goes in my pie hole, I'll be happy." Tara chuckled.

Beside him, Mo laughed and clapped him on the back. "Sounds like you'll fit in here just fine."

And though it was totally said in jest, it hit Jesse more deeply than that. One of the hardest things since retiring was feeling like he no longer belonged…anywhere. And maybe, just maybe, Tara had helped him find another way to build the foundations of a new life.

Which was just one more way Tara Hunter had rocked his world.

* * * *

Tara could hardly believe how much difference a day made. Twenty-four hours before, she'd been in the midst of the worst panic attack in months. Now, she sat surrounded by old friends and new at the end of a very good day.

And Jesse had been a big part of it.

She'd woken up with the song he'd played for her in her ear, his phone still in her hand. Despite the fact that him leaving the cell there in the first place meant he might've heard how upset she was, he'd treated her exactly the same during the whole return trip back to DC. And then he'd still wanted to check out WFC with her, and their car ride to the club had been filled with conversation and teasing—and a few seriously hot moments that made her heartrate spike every time she thought of them.

He liked looking at her? His words had made her think of him peering down his body to watch her worship his cock with her mouth which made her *need* for that to happen again. Whether her stupid brain thought it was a good idea or not.

And then there was his pronouncement that he'd take pleasure in her trying to kick his ass, which would've been hot all on its own. But it was even hotter now that she had firsthand experience wrestling with the man. She'd enjoyed that way more than she probably should've, especially since he'd bested her.

Somehow, though, feeling him wrapped around her and holding her tight, she hadn't really felt like a loser...

All of which was probably why she'd taken more time than usual to put on some makeup after she'd showered at the gym. And now, here they both were at dinner, hanging out with her friends. Noah and his girlfriend, Kristina. Billy, who was flying solo tonight because his girlfriend, Shayna, was on assignment covering a story for her job as a photojournalist for the local paper. Sean, Mo, and Dani rounded out their regular gang.

Just like at CMDS, Jesse fit in really well here with everyone. And, damnit, it felt like the two of them fit well *together*. Maybe the fact that they were co-workers wasn't that big of a deal. Then why did it feel like it was?

"So, Tara," Sean said after everyone's food had been served, "a friend of mine said good things about you earlier today."

His comment pulled her from her thoughts, and she grinned. "Uh oh." She took a bite of her fries.

"No, no, for real," he said, which was useful since Sean was such a relentless teaser. You couldn't hold it against the guy, though, because he'd do anything for any of them. And Tara figured his constant sarcasm and general smart-assery was an outlet for whatever stress being a firefighter caused. "You work with Jud Taylor, right?"

Her foot started bouncing as twin reactions coursed through her. First, surprise that Jud and Sean knew one another. Second, her belly made a slow descent to the floor in anticipation of where this was about to go. "Uh, yeah. We're on the same dive team. Same one Jesse's on now, too."

Sean nodded, seemingly not picking up on her growing anxiety. "He said you pulled his southern ass out of the ocean after a diving stage came down on him."

"Wow, that sounds scary as hell," Dani said, respect plain on her face.

Tara nodded, even though her gut told her to deflect. "His 'southern ass'?"

Laughing, Sean shrugged as he cut his steak. "His words."

That sounded like Jud. "Uh, yeah, I guess. All part of the job," she managed.

"Now you sound like me," the guy said, winking at her.

Dani threw him a smirk. "When have you ever been humble, Riddick? Like, name even *one* time."

Tara chuckled, hoping it didn't sound as forced as it felt. A hand came down on her leg. She glanced to her right where Jesse sat laughing at the razzing suddenly being slung back and forth between Dani and Sean.

It didn't look like he was paying attention to Tara, but it absolutely *felt* like he was. "How long have you two been together?" Jesse asked the pair, his tone amused.

The table absolutely erupted in pandemonium. Noah and Billy burst into laughter as Sean totally gawped like a deer in headlights before launching into a full-fledged denial. Meanwhile, Dani actually *blushed*, which Tara didn't think she'd ever before seen. The two had always had a frenemies thing going on, but the past few months, it seemed to have ratcheted between them 'til it always felt like they were on the verge of fighting...or screwing each other senseless.

"We're not together, man," Sean said again, stabbing a piece of his steak.

"Hell, no, we're not," Dani agreed. Which, come to think of it, was like the first thing Tara had ever heard Dani agree with Sean about... "How the heck did you get that we were together?"

"Shit, sorry." Jesse laughed, holding up his free hand. "I, uh, I guess I thought the bickering was like, I don't know, an old married couple's schtick."

Noah's face was bright red from laughing so hard, and Billy had tears in his eyes. For his part, Mo's deep chuckle rumbled under it all.

"Uh, geez, I really stepped in it, didn't I?" Jesse said, all self-deprecating.

Which was when Tara realized that he'd asked the question on purpose, suspecting it would derail the other topic of conversation. Something warm bloomed inside her chest—gratitude, connection, affection. Under the table, she placed her hand on top of his. His fingers curled around hers in return.

Tara's heart squeezed.

"Y'all are fucksticks," Dani said. "Every one of you. And I thought I was liking you, Jesse." She pointed her knife at him.

"Newbie error," Jesse said, smiling sheepishly. "Won't happen again."

"Good plan," Sean said, crossing his arms. Which mirrored Dani's body language exactly.

Even though it sounded like Dani was joking, Tara worried that she might really be upset that Jesse had put them on the spot, and no way did Tara want her to hold that against him. So she finally put on her big-girl panties and protected him like he'd done for her. "Don't be mad at Jesse. He was only trying to change the subject because he knows that I didn't really want to talk about yesterday's rescue."

Jesse's gaze cut to her, his brow furrowed in concern. She squeezed his hand.

"Why not, T?" Mo asked, leaning his big arms against the table.

Tara shrugged and played with her water glass. "It's just...every person around this table has saved someone else's life. It's the job. And it feels weird to get praised for doing what's expected, and what anyone would do for you."

Mo nodded as he dug into his crab cake. "I get that."

"Everyone except me," Kristina said. Tara didn't know the woman who worked as an art teacher as well as Dani, but she liked her a lot. Kristina and Noah were beyond sweet together, and they'd thrown a killer Halloween party that the whole club had attended and still talked about. "But what you just said makes a lot of sense to me."

Noah raised Kris's hand to his mouth and pressed a kiss to her knuckles. "You saved me, baby. Don't ever doubt it."

Kristina leaned over and hugged Noah, but her expression was so moved that Tara suspected she'd done it to hide tears. And, wow. That was relationship goals, right there.

Which made her realize that Jesse was still holding her hand. And that Tara had been honest with the group...and was fine. Her foot was still. Her anxiety had eased off.

"Sorry, T. Didn't mean to make you uncomfortable. Just, my buddy seemed damned impressed."

"Don't worry about it, Sean. How do you know Jud, anyway?" She gave Jesse's hand one last squeeze, and then pulled away so she could pick up her chicken sandwich. Jesse squeezed her thigh before he withdrew, a little gesture that struck her as both sweet and sexy.

"Our paths crossed in the navy," Sean said. "We've gotten together a few times since we both landed in DC. But the kicker was he emailed me to ask if I'd ever heard of WFC, because one of his teammates invited him. Don't know why I didn't think to invite him myself."

Tara nodded around a bite. "Yeah, as soon as his foot's healed up, he's going to come check it out."

After that, the conversation turned to Kristina's teaching, an interesting case Billy was investigating in his work as a private detective, and Mo's job search. And though Tara listened and participated, she couldn't stop thinking about what Jesse had done for her.

In truth, what he'd done for her again and again. Taken care of her. Protected her. Been there for her in a way no one had in a long time.

It made her want things she was scared to want. But that didn't make her desire any less.

Chapter 14

"Thanks for taking me today," Jesse said as he and Tara crossed the garage in her building toward the elevator. "It's good to have a way to meet some new people here."

Tara smiled up at him as she pressed the call button. Tonight was the first time he'd ever seen her wear makeup, and of course she was a total stunner. Then again, he didn't need her in makeup to see her that way. "I'm glad you came and that you liked it."

They stood side by side. Waiting. And for Jesse, wanting. This day with Tara had done absolutely nothing good for his interest in and desire for her. He was trying hard to respect her wishes, even though denying what was going on inside him felt so damn wrong.

She made him feel like he'd never really known warmth until he felt her sun. Like he'd never really been able to see until he stood awash in her light. Like he'd never realized he'd been locked from heaven itself until she handed him the keys and guided him inside.

The elevator doors slid open, and they stepped in. Tara pushed the buttons for the lobby and her floor.

It was crazy—utterly goddamned crazy—that this was happening to him, and for the first time at the age of thirty-seven, and after he'd only known her for a little over a week. He knew none of it made sense.

But all of that just made him even more certain and feeling even more urgent about claiming this amazing person he'd found and holding on tight. Jesus, he was in a bad fucking way where Tara Hunter was concerned.

He heaved a deep breath.

"You okay?"

A single nod. "Yeah."

They passed the last floor before the lobby. Almost time for him to leave her again. Which he didn't want to do.

Fuck it. "Tara—"

"Jesse—" She began at the same time.

"You first," he said, his heart suddenly pounding in his chest. Because she was either about to put him *all* the way back in his place—or she wasn't. And that...that he could work with.

The bell *dinged*, and the doors slid open to the lobby. Facing Tara, Jesse stood stock still.

"No," she said with a small, nervous smile. "It's nothing."

The door slid shut, and he did nothing to catch it. "The truth, always. Right?"

Her chin dropped, but she nodded. "Right." The elevator headed up again. "It's just that, uh, I realized I didn't actually know what I wanted to say."

Jesse stepped closer, close enough to smell the fragrance of berries in her hair. "About what?"

One shoulder just barely lifted in a shrug. "About...not knowing if I can have or should have what I want." The words spilled out in a rush until she just shook her head. The bell *dinged* their arrival to the eleventh floor.

Her words were uncomfortable and hopeful all at the same time, like she'd put her hand in his chest and now he'd find out if she'd done it to rip the useless organ out or hold it together. He tipped her chin up again, because he needed to see her when she answered this. "What do you want?"

The doors slid open, but she didn't move. This time, Jesse caught the elevator before it closed. After a few seconds, an alarm buzzed.

Jesse leaned in until he almost could've rested his forehead on hers. *Come on, Tara.* "What do you want?" he whispered.

"What were *you* going to say?" she asked.

He shook his head and arched an eyebrow. "Tell me what you want first."

She met his gaze head on. And she was so damn beautiful that it made him hurt with want. "You."

Jesse was hard in an instant. Hard and fucking victorious. "Jesus,

Tara, you can have me any damn time. *That's* what I was going to say."

One moment, she seemed torn and contemplative, and the next, Tara was all over him. He caught her around the waist with one arm as their mouths claimed one another, and then he was hauling her legs up around his hips so he could carry her out of the elevator.

Her hands were in his hair and her breasts pressed to his chest and her hips wiggled where his hands grasped her ass. Her actions were nearly frantic, like she was a live electric current he was trying to harness.

"Eleven twenty," she rasped.

"I remember," he said, arriving at her door. "Key?"

"In the pocket of my bag." He fished for it with one hand until he was straining and she was laughing. "Put me down so I can get it."

"No fucking way. I just got you in my arms again." Finally, he found it, and he dangled it in front of her, goddamned proud of himself.

"My hero," she said, leaning in for another kiss. And then another. And another. Her tongue slid over his so fucking good. And then she was sucking on his and rolling her hips against him and nearly taking him to his knees.

"Tara?" he managed around the edge of a kiss.

"Hmm?"

"How well do you know your neighbors?"

Her expression went comically confused. "Uh, not that well. Why?"

"Because in about ten seconds, I'm going to fuck you against this door unless we get inside."

"Oh," she breathed. Biting down on her lip, she gave him the sexiest damn smile. "That would actually be insanely hot, but, uh, not very neighborly."

Jesse grinned. "Baby, what's about to happen isn't going to be very fucking neighborly either." He finally got the key in the lock and let them inside.

Tara pushed the door closed behind them as they stumbled into the dark apartment. She dropped her bag, and he dropped his. "That way," she said. "That way's the bedroom."

"Now you're talking."

Her laughter lit him up inside. It really fucking did.

He cleared the threshold to her room, and she hit a light switch, illuminating a small lamp next to the queen-sized bed. Her room was all blues and greens, and a little bowl of sea glass sat under the glow of the lamp. Jesse was curious as hell to learn more about the woman by exploring her space, but *later.*

Mouths locked in a hungry kiss, he finally placed her on her feet. She moaned as their hands began a fumbling, hurried undressing that finally made them both laugh. Jesse tugged off his shirt, then hers, and then they both ditched their jeans, until there was nothing between them but skin and possibility.

"Condoms are in that drawer," she said, pointing to the nightstand.

"Yes, ma'am." He dumped a bunch out on the table top.

Tara grinned. "Got big plans, huh?"

He took his cock in hand and stroked, loving the way her eyes flared as she watched him. "Big fucking plans." He crooked a finger and beckoned her to him. And when she was right in front of him, Jesse went to his knees. "Starting with this."

He kissed her belly, her hip bone, her thighs, until she was gasping and bracing herself on his shoulders. "Jesse."

Tapping the inside of her thigh, he peered up at her. "Open up for me, Tara."

The moment she did, he buried his face against her. Grasping her ass in one hand, he plunged his tongue between her folds, finding her already wet and needy. But he wanted more of her—all of her. So he urged one leg over his shoulder so he could reach every part of her.

Tara's fingers dug into his shoulders, and the groan that spilled out of her sounded so good his cock jerked. "O-oh my God," she rasped.

He opened his mouth around her clit and sucked and sucked. Teased her opening with his tongue. Added two fingers and stroked at a sweet spot inside her that made her gasp and moan and go up on her tippy toes. He worked her faster and harder and deeper until her whines became beautifully urgent—and then she was holding her breath and finally squeezing his fingers so fucking tight. She came on a high-pitched cry he would never forget.

When Jesse eased his fingers from her, she collapsed into his lap. He cradled her there, loving how fast her heart beat beneath where he pressed his hand to her chest. "Feel you fly, Tara."

She grasped his face and kissed him, and though there was without question a sexiness about the way she used her tongue and her lips to tease him, it felt deeper than that, more weighted. When she pulled away, she reached over his shoulder, grabbed a condom, and opened it.

And then she put it on.

"Fuck, I see you have some big plans, too," he said. Her sexy blues flashed up from where she handled him, and she nodded. "Yeah. Straddle my lap."

Arms around his neck, she came down on top of him, impaling herself on his length until she'd taken every inch. "God, you feel good inside me."

"Ride me however you need, baby." And she did, slow and deep at first, and then faster, shallower, until she was grinding herself against him. He gripped her hips, helping her get the friction she needed. His orgasm was barreling down his spine, but he gritted his teeth because he wanted her to come again first. "That's it. Take what you need."

She was whining and babbling and tightening around him, and he fisted his hand in her hair and nipped at her neck.

"Harder," she cried.

Jesse would never hear that word again without remembering this moment. But he didn't know if she meant his teeth on her skin or his hold on her hair or his cock filling her deep, so he gave her more of all three.

"Like this?" He bit down on the tendon sloping from her neck.

He didn't need her to tell him. Because she screamed and shuddered, her body fisting his cock so fucking tight that he couldn't hold back. Hammering himself up into her as deep as he could get, Jesse's orgasm had him shouting her name and clutching her to him as his body jerked against hers. And even after his orgasm had settled, he rocked his hips, moving his cock inside her because he didn't want this to end.

This moment. This night. This feeling.

Love. He was fucking falling in love with Tara.

Even though he knew she was debating if this should even be happening at all.

Chapter 15

Tara wasn't sure what the hell she was doing. She only knew that it felt really freaking good. Not just the sex, which had once again been mind-blowing, but the connection, the companionship, affection.

"Hey," he said, pressing a little kiss to her forehead.

"Hey," she said back, smoothing her hands over the back of his neck.

Jesse helped her up, and then they took turns in the bathroom. When she came out, he was sitting on the edge of her bed, his clothes piled in his lap. "Should I go?" he asked, echoing her words from that first night.

She hated that there was even the tiniest moment of question in her gut. But there was. For now, though, she ignored the hell out of it. "Stay." He pulled her to sit sideways on his lap, making her laugh. "This was how we got in trouble the last time."

"Baby, if that was trouble it was the good kind." The smile he gave her was so damn sexy. And, *gah*, the term of endearment was too.

"Yeah," she conceded. "It was really good."

"Tara, I know…" He tilted his head so he could look her eye to eye. "I know you're not sure about me—"

"No." She shook her head, hating that he thought that. "My uncertainty is not about you, Jesse." Doubt darkened his eyes. She needed to make him believe. "It's not. I promise. It's about the fact that I struggle with anxiety—as I know you witnessed the other night—and, oh—" Her thought died mid-stream because she realized she hadn't yet thanked him for what he did. So she cupped his jaw and kissed him. Once, twice.

"What was that for?"

"For what you did for me. Your phone with the song. Being there but also giving me space. Thank you."

"You're welcome." He dipped his chin. "Was worried about you."

"I was worried about me, too. And that's at the root of why I feel any uncertainty at all. Ever since my accident, I've struggled with anxiety and panic attacks. They've gotten a lot better, and I have coping mechanisms that work pretty good. But my accident happened at work, on a dive, and it took me a long time to get myself back in the water. The idea of letting myself be distracted for even a second just…it doesn't do good things for my anxiety." Admitting all this unleashed a shiver down her spine.

Jesse reached behind him, grabbed the chenille afghan folded at the foot of her bed, and draped it around her. Taking care of her one more time. "I understand what you're saying, and I appreciate you explaining it. But we worked together all week. We worked good together."

He wasn't wrong, but there was more to it than that. "We did. I know. But I also know that I was worried about you when you skipped your safety stop. And after Jud descended, my mind kept straying to how you were doing. And even though I would've been worried about any of my teammates, my concern was deeper because it was *you*."

He listened intently as she spoke, and finally nodded. "I hear you."

"How did you feel when I went in after Jud?"

His whole expression shifted, and it was answer enough.

"See what I mean?"

Jesse laced his fingers between hers and squeezed her hand. "Not because I doubted your ability. I didn't, not even for a second."

"I believe you. But you felt different about it than if it would've been someone else, didn't you?"

"Fuck," he said, rolling them backward so that they lay close together, on their sides facing each other, their arms and legs all tangled under the blanket.

The disappointment in his voice squeezed her heart. "I know. I'm sorry. My brain's stupid now."

"Don't apologize. And nothing about you is stupid, Tara. Your feelings are totally valid." He stroked her waves back from her face. Tucked them behind her ear. Trailed his touch down her neck until his fingers traced both of her scars. The intimacy of it unleashed goosebumps all over her body. "Will you tell me what happened?"

She nodded, not because she felt like she owed him this story, though she did feel that, too. But she wanted to tell him this because, again and again, he made her feel safe to share the most vulnerable parts of herself. "My team was inspecting damage on a bridge along a critical transport route, and I was in about thirty feet of water inspecting the pilings. One of the supports collapsed, taking out part of the bridge and raining all kinds of debris down on us. A shard of broken cable caught me on the throat. It was a total, freakish, wrong place/wrong time thing. Turned out the bridge's cable system was completely corroded."

Jesse's thumb stroked her cheek as she spoke. "Jesus, Tara, that must've been terrifying."

"The crazy thing is that I don't remember most of it now, except for the *feelings*. The confusion, the fear, the panic, the pain…" She swallowed hard against the memory of those emotions, which threatened to stir as she gave them voice. But there was a strength in sharing this with someone else—she totally saw that now that she was doing it. So she kept going. "The blood loss was pretty catastrophic, as you can imagine. Our medic had to do an emergency trach in the field because I couldn't breathe. And I flatlined twice on the life-flight to base. Three other guys on my team were also injured."

"A lot of people never would've been strong enough to get back in the water after that. And no one would think the worse of them for it, either. You're so damn brave, Tara. Do you know that?"

His words helped heal parts of herself that even she sometimes picked at—the parts she thought should be *stronger*, the parts that shouldn't be bothered by this anymore, the parts at which she wanted to shout, *You survived! Get over it!*

"I don't feel brave. I certainly didn't after Jud's accident. I totally fell apart."

"Was that your first rescue since your accident?"

The fact that he guessed that said so much about how well he got her. "Yeah."

"Shit," he said. "No wonder. But don't you forget for one second that you did your job. You got him out. The adrenaline crash after something like that is a bitch all on its own. Not a soul would blame you for that impacting you the way it did."

"Thanks," she said. She waved at her eyes, blinking as she struggled to hold back tears. "It's just, women can't do this on the job. Not in these kinds of jobs, anyway. And not in front of the men they work with. Women can't be soft or emotional, because it gets read as being weak and irrational. And now that I have this anxiety going on, too, I always feel like I need to keep myself under the strictest control."

Jesse nodded, his expression full of understanding. "That's a lot of pressure for anyone."

God, she felt as disappointed as he sounded. Was she wrong here? Maybe she was making more out of this than she needed to. Maybe he was right, that despite the concern they'd sometimes felt for each other, they'd both been professionals who'd done their jobs. Maybe being involved with a teammate wouldn't be the distraction she feared and wouldn't impact how the rest of the team viewed her. *Maybe, maybe, maybe…*

Tara blew out a shaky breath, still uncertain but not wanting to be, damnit. "Maybe I could try—"

Jesse spoke at the same time. "I'll happily be just friends if—"

Both froze mid-sentence.

Tara gave a little chuckle. "We're a mess, aren't we?"

He shook his head. "No, we just found each other at the wrong time."

Those words made it feel like she was swallowing around a knot. "I could be wrong, Jesse. Maybe we could try."

Running his fingers through her hair, he frowned. "I don't want you to change for me, Tara. And I don't want you to do a single thing that would shake your confidence or make you second-guess yourself. You've been through enough. And I'm not worth it."

Her mouth dropped open and her heart hurt to hear him say such a thing. "Why would you say that?"

"Because it's true." The sadness in his dark eyes squeezed her throat. "I have a bad habit of letting people down, and I don't want you to sacrifice for me knowing I'll let you down, too, sooner or later—"

"Don't say that. I don't believe that," she said, nailing him with a stare.

"Why not? It's true. And truth is what we give each other, always. Remember?" No matter what he said, everything inside her railed against his words, but he didn't give her the chance to refute them. "So we'll see each other at work and we'll be friends." Jaw tight, he stroked her hair again, quiet for a long moment. "You can always count on me having your back."

She wanted to keep arguing with him, to challenge the way he talked about himself, but his eyes had gone distant, like he'd stepped behind a wall. And maybe she didn't have the right to push him on this when she was the one calling them off. So she just burrowed into his chest, her face against his skin. "If you'd rather not, I'll understand. But...do you want to stay the night with me?"

"Of course I do." He wrapped his arm around her shoulders and pulled her in tight.

Tara tried to remember everything about this moment. The crisp smell of his soap in her nose. The soothing strokes of his fingertips against her scalp. His heartbeat in her ear. The heat of his legs entwined with hers.

She traced a finger around one of his star tattoos, then another, and another.

All the while knowing she'd never get to be with him like this again. And it was her own damn fault.

* * * *

Two weeks had passed since Jesse had walked out of Tara's apartment in the gray light of dawn.

Two weeks had passed of them working together. The first week laying a small section of power cables under the Anacostia River. The second, inspecting bridge pilings for a newly expanded bridge in the lower Potomac River—a project they'd be continuing next week.

And fuck if Tara hadn't turned out to be right.

Because worrying about how she was feeling about doing bridge inspection work after what she'd told him had tied his gut in knots all week. Especially because Jud's foot was still bothering him, so he'd served as Tara's standby which meant she had to be in the water sharing the inspection work with Jesse. All the while, he'd had anxiety *for* her—knowing that she was having to face doing the same work that'd nearly killed her once before.

Of course, she'd handled herself like a fucking champ, because she was a professional, brilliant, and one of the bravest people he'd ever known. And that was saying something given all the people he knew who played with bombs for a living.

For the first and only time since he'd kissed her sleeping forehead and left her apartment knowing he'd lost his shot with her for good, he'd even been a little happy that they weren't together. He was already worried about how she was handling the stress of the inspection, but he knew it would've been worse for her if she'd actually had to see his concern in their private moments together, or feel it in his embrace, or taste it on his lips.

The problem was all *him*.

Jesse's heart had made some decisions all on its damn own, and now he was stuck with emotions he shouldn't have and that were getting in the way. Emotions that were keeping him from reacting to her the way he would any of his other colleagues. Emotions he needed to stuff back in the fucking box they'd come from. Except that shit couldn't be willed.

So he'd been attempting to keep things strictly professional between them.

The day they'd learned that their next job would be the bridge inspection, she and Jud had invited him out for dinner, and Jesse had passed rather than risk making clear his concern for her. He'd skipped Warrior Fight Club last Saturday because he hadn't had a chance to get his doctor to sign off on the paperwork—a handy excuse for avoiding an opportunity to get physical with her again, even in the name of exercise. And when they'd been living aboard the *Going Deep* during the bridge project, Jesse had only let himself play poker with her one night, because one night was all it took to realize he had no poker face when he was around her.

Her asking him if he was okay during the game was proof enough of that.

So distance had to be the name of the game.

Sitting on the edge of his bed on Saturday morning, he debated what to do with himself for the weekend. What he probably should do was start apartment hunting in earnest. He'd lived in this suite for a month now. It was time. Especially when he knew that part of the reason he hadn't much looked yet was because it would mean moving away from Tara.

Which was idiotic on many levels. He was well aware of that.

Except when he looked around this room, he saw them stumbling through his door, breathless and wanting. He heard her laughter in his ears from when he'd thrown her over his shoulder and onto the bed. He felt her when he lay on that mattress—the memory and the loss of her.

Fuck, if there was one thing Jesse Anderson was good at, it was torturing himself. He knew that to be true. But because some part of him believed he deserved the torturing, he always found it freaking difficult to stop.

"Fine," he said to the empty room. "Let's find a damn apartment."

His cell buzzed where it sat on the nightstand. Jesse grabbed it and found Jud's name on the screen. "Hey, Jud," he said by way of answering.

"Jesse, how are ya?"

"I'm good. What's up?" The question came out more curtly than he'd intended, and he winced.

Jud didn't seem to notice. "I think my foot's feeling up to checking out Warrior Fight Club today. You in?"

Oh. No. "Uh, I might…be busy." *Way to sell it, Jesse.*

"Too busy for me? I'm hurt, dude. Get un-busy because you're coming."

Jesse chuckled despite himself. "I'm not sure that's how this works."

"Sure it is. Be my wingman."

Exasperated, Jesse got up and paced. "What the hell do you need a wingman for?"

"Be. My. Wingman."

Raking a hand through his hair, Jesse shook his head. "But you know people there."

"Jesse, my man. When wingman duties call, the only honorable thing to do is answer that call."

Heaving a deep breath, Jesse caved. "Yeah, yeah, all right."

"Good deal. Okay, when and where is this shindig, again?" Jud's tone was so satisfied that Jesse wanted to smash his head into a wall for giving in. Seeing Tara at WFC was way the hell against his best judgment.

Jesse gave him all the information. "Bring clothes for after if you want to go out for dinner," he said, a weird hollowness filling his gut. Because it would be hard as fuck to find his way out of going along.

When they hung up, Jesse tossed his cell on the bed. It was only ten in the morning, so he could still spend part of the day making headway on his living arrangements. Which would be a better use of his time than sitting around wallowing like the morose motherfucker he'd been lately. So he opened his laptop, browsed for an online realty site, and began searching.

He was open to both apartments and houses, and he definitely wanted to buy. Between how much of his military income he'd saved over the past twenty years and his pension, he had more than enough savings to get something comfortable, even in DC.

Except, house shopping was a surefire way to remind yourself of everything you didn't have.

Master bedroom with his and her walk-in closets! Master bath with dual sinks! Awesome, except he had no one with whom to share that kind of space.

Great school district! Fanfuckingtastic, except he had no family.

Close to a metro stop and a dog park! Yipdeedamndoo, except he didn't even have a fucking dog.

At least he could do something about that last one.

Needing to make at least one thing about his life feel less empty, Jesse clicked away from his house hunt and searched for the city's SPCA. He scrolled through both the available cats and the dogs and instantly knew this was something he wanted to do.

And he didn't want a puppy or a kitten either, cute as those were.

He wanted the pets no one else wanted. The ones who wouldn't get adopted. The ones who'd been discarded or left behind by a thoughtless fucking family.

The ones who didn't fit in anywhere and had no place to call home.

The ones, well, sorta like him.

Which meant he needed to find a fucking house. One close to a dog park, thank you very much.

So he sucked it up and went back to his house hunt. And ignored the hell out of those his-and-hers closets and dual sinks he was never going to need.

Chapter 16

Tara sat in the middle of a big group of friends all having dinner and sharing their lives, and yet she'd never felt more alone in her life. Which had nothing to do with any of them, of course, and everything to do with the fact that she'd let fear dictate her life and as a result had pushed away something she'd realized too late that she wanted.

Jesse.

She missed him so much her chest actually hurt.

Maybe that was crazy given that she'd seen him almost every day for the past two weeks. But there was a wall between them now, one she'd built with her fear and her doubts. So she saw him, but she had no idea how he was doing. She worked with him, but they didn't joke around. She heard him, but he didn't say anything beyond the necessary work logistics and basic pleasantries. She got near him, but never got to touch him.

It was as if they'd never shared anything personal at all. As if they were just co-workers like any others. No, scratch that, there was now far more distance between her and Jesse than there was between her and any of her other teammates.

Which had brought her to a stunning conclusion.

There was no going backward for them. No being just friends.

And here was another revelation. She didn't really want to just be his friend, anyway.

The morning Boone had told them about the bridge inspection job, Tara had felt like the whole world sucked in on her. She spent her weekend doing her five things over and over again until she drove herself freaking nuts.

But then…she'd finished her first day on the job. She'd done it—beaten her fear. Beat it despite the fact that she and Jud had switched positions while his foot finished healing, meaning she'd been in the water with Jesse as one of the working divers. In the end, she'd realized that *anticipating* doing the work had been much scarier than actually doing it. And learning that made her feel like she was on top of the world.

Her first instinct had been to go to Jesse and celebrate with him.

But she couldn't.

And not sharing it with him made her realize there was a hole in her life—a Jesse-shaped hole. Being willing to fight her fears didn't get rid of all their challenges, but she was ready to try, to at least explore if they could be together. More than that, realizing that her first instinct was to go to Jesse made her realize that they also couldn't go back to being just friends—because she didn't feel just friendly about him.

What exactly she felt, she wasn't sure. But there were feelings there. Oh hell yes, there were. Yet she'd chased away the man those emotions were blooming toward without even realizing she was feeling them.

Because her fear had blocked everything else out like a storm cloud over the freaking sun.

The cumulative effect of all of these too-late revelations was that she felt utterly alone, even though she was sitting across the same table from Jesse. Maybe even *because* he was here. His presence should've made her happy—and it *was* good to see him, always—but what Jesse being here most did was hold up in front of Tara the amazing possibility she'd thrown away.

And, oh, God, on top of it all, he'd thought that he wasn't worth her fighting her fears for. When, without him, she might never have realized that she was stronger than her fears ever were.

Or, at least, she *could* be. If only she was as brave as he believed her to be.

So tell him you were wrong.

Tara peered across the table at him. He was laughing at some story Sean and Jud were telling, his demeanor open, easy, engaged. God, he was sexy and interesting and so freaking gorgeous.

Out of the corner of his eye, Jesse caught her looking. He did a doubletake, his brow cranking down as if in question. And all that open easiness bled right out of his expression. Finally, he looked away.

She had to tell him. Tonight. After dinner.

Having decided that, Tara was beyond happy when it finally wrapped up.

"You okay?" Dani asked when they'd all gotten up from the table.

Tara knew she hadn't been herself throughout the meal, but she just hadn't been able to help it. Through the first half she'd been all stuck in her own head, and through the second, she'd been too eager to get the hell out of there. "Yeah, just have some things on my mind." She waved a hand. "Work stuff."

"Well, if you need to talk, give me a call, okay? I know our schedules don't always jive, but we could go to dinner or a movie or something."

Smiling, Tara nodded. "I'd like that, Dani."

They spilled out of the restaurant into the chilly March night air, and everyone called out good-byes as they scattered for their cars. "Okay, I'll text you my schedule and let's set something up."

"Perfect," Tara said, truly looking forward to getting to know Dani even better. Clearly, Tara needed to make more of an effort to build a community for herself.

Which brought her thoughts back to Jesse. Scanning the parking lot, she saw him at the far side getting into his Jeep. His lights came on as he started it up.

Damnit!

She'd wanted to talk to him, but he'd beelined out of there like he was escaping enemy waters. Tara's shoulders sagged as she got into her own car, backed out, and pulled into the street.

Which was when she realized Jesse was two cars ahead of her, waiting at the light. It wasn't like she didn't know where he lived…

She might've felt like a bit of a creeper following him across town if he hadn't been going the exact same way she was, especially when she floored it on a yellow light so they didn't get separated. Now that she'd determined to talk to him, she was nearly coming out of her skin to do it as soon as she could.

Now. She wanted him to know she wanted him now.

He turned onto the street with access to the Marriott's garage. Tara had two choices—to go home and walk back over, or…

Jesse turned into his garage. Tara turned in after him.

Butterflies performed a whole freaking aerial show in her belly. If Jesse hadn't realized before that she'd been following him on purpose, he sure as hell did now.

The worst thing was she didn't know how he was going to react to her, proving that, once again, the anticipation of what you feared was worse than the thing itself. At least, she sure as hell hoped that would be true here.

Two levels down, he parked, passing several available spots in favor of one that had free spaces adjacent to it. Perfect. She pulled in right next to him, killed her engine, and looked to her right—to find Jesse staring at her wearing an expression she couldn't read.

He got out. So did she.

"What's going on, Tara?" he asked. *Wary.* That was the only way to describe him—his tone, his posture, the look in his eyes.

Stomach doing a flip, Tara met him at the back of his car. "I need to talk to you."

He leaned back against his Jeep, stance wide, arms crossed. Like he was resigned but not happy about it. "Okay."

Wasn't going to make this easy for her, was he? Fair enough. She was the one who'd put them through this after all. She forced a deep breath, debated for the space of a second what to say, and then let the words fly. "I made a mistake."

"About what?"

"About us."

He shook his head. "No, you didn't."

She frowned. "I'm pretty sure I know how I feel, Jesse, and I—"

"How do you feel?" Oh, man, the walls were up so high behind those dark eyes.

Her words spilled out in a heartfelt rush. "I miss you. I realized I let myself be ruled by fear, and I'm angry at myself about that. And most of all I have feelings for you that are beyond friendship."

Jesse swallowed so thickly his Adam's apple bobbed in his throat. "I have feelings for you, too, Tara. But nothing's changed."

His words both lifted her up and threatened to crash her to earth again. "Everything's changed."

"Like what?" he said, suddenly raking at his hair.

"Like I have feelings for you. And I'd like the opportunity to explore them with you. To see where we can go. I don't want to let fear and anxiety rule the rest of my life. But I do want you."

He frowned, and it made her stomach drop to the floor. "The thing is, Tara, I've had the chance to do a lot of thinking these past two weeks, every bit of which adds up to one thing—you were right."

"But, Jesse—"

"This bridge inspection…" He shook his head as if he were gathering the word-bricks to build his wall even higher. "Jesus, Tara, you were *right*. I don't look at you the same way I look at the others. I *can't*. Because having feelings for you means that my head knows you're as good as anybody else on the team, but my fucking heart hurt for you knowing what this job was putting you through. But I couldn't let you know that, because I didn't want to make it worse."

That was why he'd been so distant? Because he was worried to show that he cared? Cautious hope rose in her chest. "But we did our jobs, just like you said. And I beat my fear of this stupid project."

"You did. And I was really fucking proud of you. But that doesn't change the basic premise of the problem you laid out. Nothing's changed."

She laid a hand to her chest. "I've changed."

His eyes were so sad that she felt his pain. "I haven't."

"Are you saying this because you think you're not worth me fighting for? Because you are, Jesse, you are worth fighting for. To me," she said around a sudden tightness in her throat.

He ignored her question. "I'm saying this because it's true."

Her stomach tossed. Her hands got shaky. Her chest tightened. She knew what these signs meant—something was scaring her. Badly. And it made her desperate to put an end to her fear. "Then I'll…I'll look for another job."

Jesse pushed off his Jeep and came right at her, a storm of emotion rolling across his face. "No fucking way."

Tara held her ground. "Why not?"

He nailed her with a stare. "Because you'll regret it. And then someday you'll resent me. And I'm not worth it—that much you'll have to take my word for."

"I don't believe you, Jesse. I don't know why you feel that way. But you'll never convince me."

On a sigh, he planted his hands on his hips. "Tara…"

She shook her head, mentally pushing away every one of his arguments, because they all added up to an outcome she no longer wanted. Them, apart. "But what about us?"

Jesse's expression softened, and he stroked his knuckles down her cheek. He gave her a small, sad smile. "We'll always have Paris."

Sudden hot tears spilled from her eyes. He'd just slid the sweetest knife right into her heart. But if he said Rick's *here's looking at you, kid* line, she was going to legit sob. "Don't quote *Casablanca* to me now."

"I'm sorry," he said, catching her tears with his thumb. "About all of it."

Tara turned away and wiped at her face. But the stupid tears wouldn't stop spilling, as if they were the only way her heart could release the pressure squeezing it inside her chest.

Big hands settled on her shoulders from behind. Jesse kissed the top of her head. "Do you want me to drive your car over to your place for you?"

Her breath caught. She turned in his embrace, but he dropped his hands to his sides. "But…" She didn't know what she'd been about to say, just that she didn't want this to be the end. Finally, she shook her head. "No, I can manage getting home."

"Okay."

The only thing Tara knew in that moment was that she couldn't watch him walk away. So she got in her car and left him standing there.

Don't look back, don't look back.

But of course she did, finding him in her rear-view mirror still standing in the same spot, arms crossed, head hanging.

All the possibility between them finally gone, once and for all.

Chapter 17

Jesse had never been so fucking grateful to get off a boat in his life. The *Going Deep* came into their marina on Thursday evening, the bridge inspection project complete.

And that meant two very important things—one Jesse hated, and one he was potentially excited about.

The thing he hated was that part of him was glad to get some space from Tara. They'd gotten through the week without anyone else being the wiser. But ever since their conversation last Saturday night, Jesse had felt like he was a walking open wound that he didn't know how to close.

Seeing her hurt. Hearing her hurt. Accidentally touching her hurt. Hell, seeing *her hurt* goddamned hurt. So, frankly, he was glad for her to have some time apart from him, too.

She was right. They were a mess.

And, for him, she was another brutal loss to add to all the ones that'd come before, tearing yet another hole in him until he feared he wasn't a whole man. How many pieces could he possibly have left to lose? Because even though he and Tara should've had everything going for them, there was an immovable obstacle still standing in their way. And fuck but it was hell learning that sometimes love wasn't enough.

Because he had that. He fucking had that in spades.

And still he couldn't make a relationship work.

The thing that he was potentially excited about had hit his email on Monday. A personal invitation to a recruitment event for veterans with Metro Police, which was expecting an opening on the bomb squad within their Special Operations Division following the retirement of the squad's long-time commander late this spring. Jesse had submitted an interest card through their website months ago and had forgotten all about it after he'd accepted CMDS's offer.

Was Jesse interested in being considered for the position?

Hell, yes, he was.

If he got the job, it would obviously cause some challenges for his current situation. He'd feel bad for leaving Boone, and he sincerely hoped the man would understand because Jesse had already grown to like and respect him. But maybe, just maybe it would also solve some even bigger problems. Jesus, maybe even the biggest problem he'd ever had in his life.

The problem of loving Tara Hunter.

Since they'd returned to DC a day earlier than expected, Jesse could attend the first day of the recruitment event tomorrow instead of waiting until Saturday.

Small victories, but man, he'd take 'em where he could find 'em.

The team got the *GD* docked and cleaned up, stowed all their equipment, and said their good-byes to Mama D. And then Jesse headed out into the lengthening light of evening like work had been a jail and he was a newly freed man.

Fuck, this hope was so goddamned dangerous to be feeling. There were about a hundred things that needed to happen before he'd be remotely justified feeling it, but nobody ever accused the heart of being rational. Lately, his had been entirely out of fucking control.

Now, maybe he could do something about it.

He paused to unlock his car door, and something made him look up. He shouldn't have been surprised to find Tara looking at him, because they were like magnets, only right now they were set to repel.

He gave her a nod, and she attempted a smile.

Hold on for me, Tara.

Sending that thought to her was all he could do for now. Raising his own hope was one thing. Raising hers would be unforgivable if he couldn't deliver on it.

So he was at the recruitment event at a DC hotel first thing the next morning dressed in a brand new suit he'd bought off the rack the night before. Since he'd RSVPed, they were expecting him. And since he'd submitted his experiences, qualifications, and personal statement one night from the *Going Deep*, he was directed to a partitioned conference room.

A uniformed officer rose and shook Jesse's hand. "I'm Officer Landers with the SOD, uh, the Special Operations Division."

"Hello, sir, I'm Jesse Anderson."

The man gestured to the seat opposite his at the table. "Please sit while I pull up your application materials." He scrolled through some information on an iPad and finally nodded, an increasingly impressed look on his dark brown face. "Twenty years in the navy, rising to the rank of chief petty officer. Over a dozen years EOD, with leadership positions in more than one of the navy's mobile EOD units. Special warfare training. These are impressive credentials, Mr. Anderson."

"Thank you."

"What makes you interested in Metro PD?" The officer gave him an appraising look.

"Sir, I retired from the navy a little over a year ago. During the two years before that, I lost eight of my men." Admitting this felt a lot like swallowing crushed glass, but it was the truth. And his fear that their loss represented a failure of his leadership was something he'd been thinking a lot about the past week. Because of something Tara had said.

I don't want to let fear and anxiety rule the rest of my life.

He'd replayed every part of their conversation over and over again in his head, and slowly that declaration began to stand out to him.

Because hadn't he been doing the same thing? His fear that he was bad for the EOD community. That he'd let them down. That if he stayed, he'd lead even more men to get hurt or killed.

Fuck, Tara had nearly died and managed to beat her fears. And he knew without *knowing* that she'd lost people she cared about, too. Because that was a cost of war that every single service member paid. But still she kept fighting.

Now it was time for him to fight. For himself. And so he could do it for Tara.

She thought he was worth fighting for—maybe it was time he started to believe that, too. Because he sure as hell knew that she was worth the fight.

Jesse continued, "At the time, I didn't have enough distance from those losses to understand that I hadn't caused them. This last year has given me perspective. It's made me see that every one of those men understood the danger and was prepared to sacrifice, just as I was. I currently work at a commercial diving outfit with some great people. I like the work. But it's not my passion. Being the wall between bad people and their dangerous weapons and our community—that's what I've dedicated most of my life to. And it's what I realized I still feel passionate about."

The words spilled from him like a revelation. And to him, they were. Because somehow in the midst of absolute heartbreak, he'd found a piece of himself again. And fuck if Tara hadn't given that to him—along with so much else.

The officer made some notes as Jesse talked. "Your field has the tendency to chew people up and spit them out."

"That's for sure, sir."

"Tell me about some of your special warfare training."

Jesse detailed the schools he'd gone to, the special training he'd completed, and gave an overview of some of the ops he'd been a part of, wishing he knew what the magic words were to get the man to say "you're hired," even though he knew that wasn't happening today no matter what. Like the military, law enforcement had layers of testing and screening before decisions were made.

After making some additional notes, the man put down the iPad, leaned back in his chair, and laced his fingers. "It's not often we get a candidate with quite your level of experience, not just EOD but underwater EOD, too. It goes without saying that we'd love to see you progress through the application process. You're aware that there's an upcoming opening on our bomb squad?"

Jesse nodded, more of that dangerous hope crowding into his chest.

"Would you be available next Wednesday to take the required online tests for our Experienced Officer Program?"

"Yes." Jesse would talk to Boone as soon as he was done here to get the day off.

"Assuming you perform well on those, we'd have you attend one of our upcoming Prospect Days where you'd take the physical ability test, complete the screening process, along with fingerprinting, a polygraph, and medical and psychological evaluations."

All SOP—standard operating procedure. "Understood."

"It can then take anywhere from a few days to a month for the entirety of your application to be reviewed."

A month. A rock took root in Jesse's gut. But it was better than no chance at all. "Yes, sir."

"To get just a little ahead of ourselves, our Experienced Officer Transition Program is an accelerated training at the Metropolitan Police Academy. Next one starts in April so this is opportune timing for the upcoming opening. There are separate SOD trainings you'd need, but those could be performed concurrently with an assignment to both the special tactics branch or the bomb squad."

Okay, the fact that Officer Landers was talking about these assignments as if they were likely placements felt like more reason to hope. Didn't it? Fuck, Jesse was almost restless with the need to get all of this underway. "I'm eager to get the process started as fast as I can." Understatement of the damn century right there.

The officer stood and extended his hand. They shook. "Then they'll see you Wednesday at the testing center."

Now all Jesse had to do was nail every one of these tests like they were an op and his life depended on it.

Because to him, it did.

* * * *

Jesse had been acting weird the past few weeks. Tara couldn't put her finger on why, but he hadn't been himself.

He'd missed random days of work. Seemed pensive one minute, and unusually talkative the next. Snuck glances at her like he'd done during their first week working together, back when they were trying to stay away from each other even though they'd just been a collision waiting to happen.

A fatal collision if the way her heart hurt was any indication.

It'd been almost three weeks since that awful conversation in Jesse's garage. Of course, Tara was doing what life required of her, but losing any chance at all with Jesse felt a whole lot like she was dragging around a lead blanket on her back. One that kept pressing her down and down.

God, falling in love sucked. The heart wanted what it freaking wanted whether it could have it or not. While she'd thought her one-night stand to be fun, *this* she could live the rest of her life without.

Which was why she was glad that today was Warrior Fight Club. Beating the shit out of something was exactly what she needed, even if the relief it provided would only be temporary. And it would only be temporary—she knew that. Because in the weeks since she'd pulled out of Jesse's garage, the life she'd previously led no longer made her happy. In the wake of falling in love and getting her heart broken, she often felt lonely and unsatisfied, like there was more she could be doing. *Should* be doing.

She hated feeling that way when she had a good job, enough of the things she needed, and friends in the club. She should feel grateful for all she had. And she did, of course. But…

Something needed to give.

Tara just hadn't figured out what it was yet.

So she went to fight club and found herself both relieved and disappointed that Jesse wasn't there.

"Pair off," Coach Mack called out after they'd warmed up.

Tara looked for Dani, but she'd already partnered with Noah. Sean held up his hands and grinned at her. "It's your lucky day."

Tara laughed despite herself. "Go easy on me."

"Oh, sure, and then you'll kick my ass and what will that do for my rep?"

She rolled her eyes and paid attention to Coach as he spoke again.

"We're going to practice choke holds and joint locks. One of you will be the mount, and your goal is to put your opponent in a hold and keep him there, finishing the fight. The other of you will be the guard, looking to escape the hold, which passes the guard, or reverses your position with the mount. Colby and Hawk will demonstrate different joint locks and then you'll take turns practicing them."

Tara groaned when Colby demonstrated with the ankle lock, because it relied on upper body strength, and next to Sean she had no chance.

"Mount or guard?" Sean asked.

She smirked at him. "This is a David-and-Goliath situation here."

He smirked back. "Yeah, doofus, but David won."

She appreciated the sentiment. "Okay, I'll mount then. Might as well start out on top."

They sat on the floor facing each other, and Tara pinned Sean's big-ass foot under her arm pit, using her grip on Sean's shin and the tight press of her arm to try to trap his foot. "Hold on," she said, adjusting her grip for a tighter hold.

"There you go," Sean said, tugging and twisting.

Tara held on tight as Sean attempted to break the hold, gritting her teeth as her grip started to slip. Still, she held on.

"See, T? You're tougher than you think."

She tried it a few more times, and she had to admit that it felt good to no longer be the newbie here. Her skills had improved a lot since she'd joined early last summer. Even when she got beat, she usually knew what mistake she'd made.

Annnd of course that felt like a life lesson. Tara sighed.

"Okay, my turn," Sean said, grabbing her ankle.

"Dude, your biceps are crazy. Like, if you flexed hard enough, that thing could snap my ankle."

He chuckled. "You ain't that fucking fragile."

She rolled her eyes, and he made her pay for it by twisting her leg, which forced her hips to rotate and made her roll onto her side. "Okay, asshole," she said, laughing.

The next two holds Tara enjoyed more, even if for different reasons.

She was much better than Sean at the straight armbar because she was more flexible and her smaller stature made her more agile, but she was no competition at all against his rear naked choke. Worse, he was so bulky and she was so short that it was hard to get her legs around the front of his to fully hook him into the hold. They'd both ended up laughing.

When they were done, Sean held out a hand and pulled her off the floor. "Good working with you."

"Thank you for not breaking me." She withdrew her hand.

But he held on and cocked his head. "You doing okay, T?"

"Yeah, why?"

His gaze lingered on her face until she almost wanted to squirm. Finally, he let her go and shrugged. "I don't know. Just a feeling."

Gah, she wasn't sure she could take the big lug being sweet. Her heart was too fragile for that right now. But she also didn't want to blow him off. "Well, your radar isn't wrong, but I'll be okay."

He gave a nod. "You know where to find me."

"At the firehouse?" The guy was well known for picking up overtime, so it was a safe bet.

Grinning, Sean nodded. "Almost always. But you know what I mean."

"Yeah, thanks," she said, really appreciating him looking out for her.

The rest of WFC passed in a bit of a blur. Tara just wasn't into it the way she usually was. She knew she was in a bad place when beating on things didn't make her feel better. For crap's sake.

Tara was almost relieved when it was time to clean up. While she showered, Dani told her about how her boss at work was trying to pressure her into a promotion that came with a lot more responsibility but almost no additional pay, and Tara was glad to have someone else's problems to focus on. "How can that be fair?" Tara asked.

"It isn't," Dani said from the neighboring shower stall, "which is why I turned him down."

"How did that go over?" Tara asked as she rinsed. She shut off the water and grabbed her towel.

A rueful chuckle sounded from Dani's stall. "He acted like I'd said I wanted to think about it."

"In other words, he's going to keep bugging you." Tara wrapped a second towel around her wet hair.

"Exactly." Dani's water shut off, and soon they were at their lockers in the same little hall getting dressed. "How come Jesse and Jud didn't come today?"

The question hit Tara right in the gut. "Oh, uh, I don't know."

Dani frowned. "Huh."

Don't ask, don't ask, don't ask. "What does that mean?"

Stepping into her jeans, Dani shrugged. "I guess I just thought you and Jesse were close."

Now Tara was the one shrugging—and kicking herself for asking. "I thought we might be, but it didn't work out."

Dani froze with her sweater in her hands. "Shit. Why? What happened?"

Tara turned away and made a little project of finding her shirt in the locker. "We work together. It got complicated." She couldn't help but wonder if things would've worked out the same way if Tara had agreed to give them a try the night she'd brought Jesse home to her apartment. Never know now, of course, but the second-guessing was a futile game her brain wouldn't stop playing.

A game that made her know into her very soul that she'd nearly had something amazing.

"That sucks." Dani's voice was full of sympathy. "Your team at CMDS is really small, isn't it?"

Swallowing around a sudden knot in her throat, Tara agreed. "Yeah. Anyway." She tugged a slate blue V-neck over her head, grabbed her bag, and went to the counter with the outlets.

Dani joined her, and their gazes met in the mirror. "I'm sorry about Jesse."

Opening her make-up bag, Tara nodded. "Thanks." She appreciated her friends checking in on her. She really did. But she also didn't want to talk about Jesse anymore. Didn't want to think about him. Didn't want to remember his dark eyes looking at her, his voice in her ear, his hands on her skin.

She didn't want to want him. Because, oh God, she still did.

Fifteen minutes later they were finished getting ready and walked out into the gym to join the guys so they could leave for dinner. But none of them were there yet.

"How did we get ready before them?" Dani asked. "Both of our hair is like down to our asses and we still beat them."

"I don't know," Tara said, chuckling. Then she glanced at the door and froze.

Jesse.

Jesse was standing on the other side of the windows peering in. What was he doing here? Tara's heart tripped inside her chest. And then she put the kibosh on her runaway expectations and realized that he might not be here for her at all. Just like she'd expected, he'd hit it off with Noah and Sean. So....

Right. Be cool.

Which was so not her strong suit. Obviously.

But she had to at least try, which was why she just waved and then turned away from him. She wasn't letting her stupid heart get her hopes up.

Not this time.

Chapter 18

The door swung open behind her, and like a glutton for punishment, Tara turned to see Jesse heading right for her—six-foot-two inches of confusingly determined hot man coming at her five-foot-four inches of cluelessness and heartache.

"Hey, Dani," Jesse said, his eyes locked on Tara's.

"Uh, hi, Jesse. Whatcha doing?" Dani asked, coming to stand right beside her.

"Hi, Tara," Jesse said. "Can I talk to you?"

She blinked out of her shock. "You joining us for dinner?" Because she couldn't think of any other reason he'd be there. "You missed training, so I didn't think…"

He shook his head. "No, I'm here for you."

Tara's belly did a nauseating little loop. "Uh, I don't…"

"Can I please talk to you?" he asked again, those dark eyes burning with an intensity she didn't understand. God, why did he have to be so beautiful?

"Sure," Tara finally said.

"You sure?" Dani asked.

Managing a little smile at her friend's protectiveness, Tara nodded. "Yeah, I'm good. Um, I'll just meet you at the restaurant."

Dani nodded, her gaze going from Tara to Jesse and back again. "Okay."

"Can we…is there a private place to talk here?" he asked.

"Um. There are some classrooms down the hall that might be open," Tara said mechanically as they pushed through the door leading to the hallway.

They closed themselves into the first empty room.

Tara hugged herself and turned toward Jesse. "So, uh, what's up?"

He blew out a breath and came closer. "Shit. I raced over here so fast after I heard that I forgot to plan what to say."

"Heard what?" Tara was utterly confused—not just by his words but also by the almost frenetic energy coming off of him. *Positive* energy. Gone was the distance. Gone was the wall behind his eyes.

"I got a new job. I didn't want to say anything in case it didn't come through, but—"

"Wait. What?"

His smile was so freaking beautiful. "I got a new job. I'm joining the DC Police's Special Tactics Branch as an EOD specialist."

The room spun around Tara until it felt like the floor was wavy beneath her feet. "I...but you...you said if I got a new job, I'd resent you for it. I don't want you to change jobs because of me."

Jesse grasped her gently by the arms. It was the first time he'd reached for her in weeks, and it made her ache with remembered want. "Tara, I'm doing this for me. I like CMDS, but this law enforcement position...it brings me back to what I'm passionate about. To what I didn't think I could do anymore. But I was wrong. I was wrong about so much."

"Jesse, I..." He was leaving CMDS? So now she'd almost never see him... "Um, congratulations, then," she said lamely. "Did you tell Boone yet?"

"Yes, he knew I was looking. Because of my military experience, I can do an accelerated police academy, and the next one starts April 15. I'm going to keep diving until then."

"Wow, Boone knew? How did he react?"

"Disappointed at first. Until I explained that I wanted to stop running from EOD, because that's what I'd done. I told him I needed the chance to make that right, and he understood."

Pride and respect welled inside her chest. "Jesse, that's amazing."

He nodded and stepped closer. "All thanks to you."

Tara's belly flipped, and she hugged herself. "What do you mean?"

"Watching you face your fears made me realize I wasn't facing mine, and I... Shit, I'm handling this all wrong," he said, frowning.

"Jesse—"

Suddenly, he was right in front of her, so close she had to tilt her head way back to meet his gaze. Those dark eyes absolutely blazed at her. "Tara, *fuck*. I'm just gonna say it straight out. I love you. That's where I should've started all this. I love you. I probably fell in love with you after that first nacho. If not then, when you suggested a kiss was the best cure for the cold. And if not then, definitely when you jumped into a stormy sea to save a man's life."

Tara's mouth fell open as her mind struggled to process the words she thought she was hearing. He loved her? Had he really said that?

"I'm sorry we had to go through hell to get here—or, at least, I know I did. But now you can do what you love without compromising what's important to you. And I can return to what I love. And...and we can be together. That's what I came here to say."

Her heart beat so hard and so fast that it made her head spin. "Oh, my God..."

He cupped her face in his big hands. "Fuck, did it take me too long to fight my way back to you?"

Tears sprung to her eyes as what was happening finally sank in. He loved her. Jesse loved her. And he'd made it so they could have a chance. "No," she said as the first tear fell. "Not too late."

"Aw, don't cry," he said. "I'm so fucking sorry."

She shook her head. "None of that matters, Jesse. I just...all that matters is that I love you, too."

Sheer relief. That was the only way she knew to describe the wide-eyed expression that settled onto his handsome face. "Say it again," he whispered.

More tears fell. "I love you, Jesse. So much."

He kissed her then, slow and deep, a tender reunion that made her feel like she was floating. He loved her. When the kiss ended, he pulled her in for a hug and held her so damn tight.

"Don't let me go," she whispered, needing his arms around her so much. Now and always.

"Never again." After a long moment, he released her just enough to look her eye to eye. "I know you were planning to go to dinner. Did you want to—"

"I just want to be with you."

Jesse took her by the hand. "Done, baby. Let's go home."

* * * *

They went back to Jesse's suite, because that was where it had all started.

They didn't rush. They weren't frantic. They took their time, exploring and indulging. Because they finally had a future in front of them.

When they were both naked, Jesse laid Tara out on his bed, hardly able to believe that she was his. That he'd laid all his cards out and finally won a hand. That she loved him, too.

But she did. And that…that meant everything. Hope and possibility and maybe even forever. At thirty-seven, Jesse was a man who knew what he wanted when he found it—and he had every intention of making Tara Hunter his in every way he could. When the time was right. And if she would have him. For the first time in a long time, he had hope—hope that she would.

But all that was for another time. Now, Jesse needed Tara in his arms. He settled between her soft thighs, their mouths claiming each other, their hands holding so damn tight. Being inside her felt like finally coming home, especially when she came with his name and her love for him on her lips. And he did the same.

Afterward, they lay cuddled for a long time. "Is this a dream, Tara?"

She settled her chin on his chest and smiled. "No, Jesse, this is our real life."

Out of nowhere, he got choked up. He pressed his fingers to his eyes and heaved a deep breath. It was just, he'd been alone for so long that finding Tara and being loved by her meant the world to him. Because he never thought he'd find this—this happiness. "What if I'd never run into you?"

"But we did. We found each other. And I think…" She gave a little shrug. "Now I think I believe in meant to be."

He swallowed hard. "I don't know what I did to deserve you, Tara. But I promise I'll devote my whole life to making you happy."

She crawled on top of him, bringing their faces close. "You were you. That's all you did. That's all you had to do, Jesse."

He nodded as her words reached inside him, slowly healing things that'd long been broken.

"Would you please tell me why you feel so unworthy? Because I'm going to devote my life to showing you that you're worth everything I have to give."

"Yeah," he said, struggling for the words. It was hard revealing the ugliest parts of yourself, even to the person you loved and who loved you back. "I guess it goes back to the fact that my dad and I didn't get along very well. I disappointed him a lot, and he thought I made one bad choice after another. It felt like nothing I did was ever good enough. I chose to run track instead of play hockey, which was what he'd wanted because it was the sport he'd played. He wanted me to be a surgeon, which at one point I thought I wanted, too. But when I told him I'd changed my mind and that I wanted to enlist in the navy, we had a horrible fight. He wanted me to go to college, and told me I'd be throwing my life away. That I'd have to live with that mistake. That he'd thought I was better than that, smarter. So when I left after high school, I rarely went back home to Cunningham Falls. I didn't want to rub the navy in my parents' faces. And I didn't want to see his disapproval either."

"Oh, man. I'm so sorry. I can't imagine how hard that must've been. So you never worked it out with him? He never came around?" She cupped his face in her hand.

He shook his head and played with a tendril of her hair. "He died five years ago. I went home for the funeral, and I felt so out of place there that I've only been back one other time, when my sister's husband died in a freak skiing accident." Jesse never having the chance to make things right with his dad would always be one of his biggest regrets.

"That's terrible," Tara said, sadness on her pretty face. Sadness for him. Because she was on his side. Right now, that's all that mattered. "Jesse, I'm so proud of you."

He searched her eyes, seeing nothing but sincerity. "What for?"

Tara kissed him, once, twice. "For your service. For your incredible bravery in putting yourself in harm's way again and again to do one of the most dangerous jobs in the world. At seventeen or eighteen, you knew what you wanted to devote your life to, and then you did it. And now you're about to do it again with the police. So I'm proud of you. I'm also telling you this because I'm worried that no one's ever said it to you. And you deserve to know that you're amazing."

"I fucking love you," he whispered, drawing her in for a long, lingering kiss as the emotion warmed all the cold, hard parts inside him. God, she made him feel like a new man, a better man.

When they pulled apart, Tara tilted her head. "So you really don't have a relationship with your family at all now?"

"My mom texts and calls sometimes. But I feel like…." He struggled to give voice to the mess inside him where his family was concerned. "I feel like I don't know how to be her son anymore. How to fix things after so long."

"Did she disapprove of the navy, too?" Tara asked.

"No. I mean, at first she was concerned for all the reasons any parent would be. But she saw it was what I wanted to do."

Tara grasped one of Jesse's hands and kissed his knuckles. "Then, Jesse, you don't have to *try* to do anything special to be her son. You *are* her son. And I would bet any amount of money that she would give anything to be in your life."

A rock settled into his gut. Could it really be that easy? Was this another area of his life where he'd let fear stand in the way? "You really think so?"

"I really do. When was the last time you talked to her?"

He thought back. "It's been a few weeks."

Suddenly, Tara pushed herself off him until she knelt between his knees. "Call her. Call her and tell her…just tell her that you love her."

Jesse's heart was suddenly a bass beat in his chest. He sat up and pressed his face against Tara's chest. "I'd rather play with your boobs."

She laughed and pushed him away. "Call your mom. That's an order, sailor."

"Fuck, you're tough."

She kissed him. "Better believe it."

He got up and started looking for his jeans, his mind racing.

Tara frowned. "What are you doing?"

"I can't reconcile with my mother with my junk hanging in the wind."

She laughed so hard she snorted. He did a doubletake at her and grinned. "Sorry," she said. "But I do believe your mother's seen your junk."

He smirked and threw his shirt at her. "Not for like thirty-five fucking years."

"Fair point," she said, still laughing at him. And, fuck, he didn't even mind when he knew that she was there for him, on his side, having his back. The last time he'd had that was in the military. But now he had that kind of partnership in life. And it meant the fucking world.

Finally, Jesse had his phone in hand. He went to his recent calls and pressed his mom's name. It rang. He couldn't believe he was so nervous.

"Jesse, is that you?" she said by way of answering.

He paced. "Hey, Mom. Yeah. How are you?"

The look on Tara's face was so damn hopeful. For him. She gave him a thumbs-up, and he nodded.

"I'm good, hon. Is everything okay?" The surprise in her tone killed him.

He had to make this right. "I'm fine. There's no reason to worry. But, um, I guess, in a way, no, everything's not all right."

"Tell me what's going on, Jesse."

He swallowed hard—and made a leap of faith. "Mom, I'm sorry. About everything. About not getting along with Dad and making things hard on you and Willa. About not coming home and not staying in touch. I don't want it to be like that anymore. I miss you. And Willa. And if you can forgive me, I want my family back."

"Oh, my sweet boy," his mother said, her tone full of tears. "Nothing would make me happier. I love you, Jesse."

A knot of emotion settled into his throat, and he sat on the bed. Tara hugged him from behind, and he put a hand on her knee and squeezed. This was one more thing Tara Hunter had given him. "I love you, too, Mom. And I'm sorry."

"I'm sorry, too. But now we look forward. I have so much to tell you."

Jesse looked over his shoulder to find happy tears in Tara's eyes. "There's so much I want to tell you, too…"

Which was how Jesse found out that Willa was getting married in June—to her childhood sweetheart, Max Hull. Somehow they'd found their way back to each other, and Jesse couldn't wait to hear that story straight from Willa, since he'd now be going to her wedding. Going home to Cunningham Falls. And it was how his mom learned that Jesse was in love with the most amazing woman in the world, and about to start a new job he was passionate about. And so many other things.

When he got off the phone, he turned in Tara's arms and hugged her tight. "Thank you, baby. You were right."

She held him close and kissed his cheek. "I'm so glad, Jesse. You deserve to have a family."

He tilted his head back and looked her right in the eyes. *Marry me.*

That was what was on the tip of his tongue. But he needed a ring. And he wanted to make an occasion out of it. To make it as special as this woman and the love he'd found with her. So…soon.

Instead, what he said was, "I love you, Tara."

Because for today, that was finally enough.

Epilogue

Eleven weeks later

Tara was a ball of nerves—but they were all of the good kind.

Today was Jesse's graduation from the police academy, and Tara couldn't be more proud of him. "Go get 'em, Jesse," she said, giving him a kiss as they entered the lobby of the big police academy building.

He tucked his blue uniform hat under his arm. And geez did this man look fine in the crisp dark blue dress uniform. His black shoes gleamed.

"Thanks, baby," he said, giving her one more kiss. And then he crossed the lobby to where some of the other new graduates were heading into an adjoining room. Right away, they all greeted Jesse, shaking his hand and giving him fistbumps. Tara smiled watching him, so glad he'd found a whole new group of brothers—and sisters—who'd always be there for him.

The minute Jesse disappeared, Tara got out her cell and shot off a bunch of texts. She'd planned some surprises for him and she was about coming out of her skin with the hope that she could pull them all off.

And as those surprises started to arrive, she couldn't stop grinning. Jesse deserved to know how many people cared. How much *she* cared. And she wanted nothing more than for him to feel that today.

Finally, they were all seated—taking up most of two rows in the big auditorium, Tara noted with delight. Excitement from all the recruits' gathered friends and families buzzed around the room until the ceremony began.

First, senior officers processed in down one side of the aisle, then stood in front of the first three rows of seats on the right. The mayor and police chief took places upon the stage, framed by the U.S. and DC flags.

And then the doors on the other side of the auditorium opened, and the new recruit class processed in. Eyes straight ahead, marching in step. Eighteen in all.

Jesse was second in line, and Tara couldn't take her eyes off him as he moved to the front of the room where the class stood before the first two rows of seats. After the Pledge of Allegiance, everyone sat.

The mayor spoke, then the police chief, and all the while Tara was just dying for Jesse to turn around and see who was here for him. And then the chief asked the recruits to stand with their badges in their hands and turn to face their families. The recruits recited their oath of office.

And Tara saw the exact moment when Jesse found her in the crowd—and then all the others.

Jesse's mom, his sister Willa, and his nephew Alex had flown in from out West. Ever since their reconciliation, Jesse and his mom had talked once a week, and Tara had stolen her number from his phone and called to invite the lady. They'd ended up having a wonderful chat that left Tara warmed with the knowledge of just how much Jesse's mother loved him. And despite the fact that Willa's wedding was in less than two weeks, she and her son had also made the trip. Jesse had reached out to her, too, and now they were keeping in regular touch for the first time in years.

Tara was so happy for him.

Next to his family was the whole CMDS crew, including Mama D, who'd been beside herself with joy when she'd learned that Tara and Jesse were together. She'd insisted that they join her and Boone for dinner on their sailboat, and Tara was glad that they'd been so understanding about Jesse switching jobs. Them being here to celebrate him certainly proved that.

Jesse's eyes went wider as he recited the last lines of the oath and his gaze scanned the row behind Tara. Because a bunch of Warrior Fight Club friends had come, too. Noah and Kristina, Billy and Shayna, Dani, Mo, Sean, and even Coach Mack.

Jesse's gaze snapped back to hers, full of love and amazement. Tara's cheeks hurt from grinning so big.

When the oath was over, the police chief asked the recruits to be seated, and then, recruit by recruit, she invited family members to come forward to pin their new badges on their uniforms.

"Officer Jesse Anderson."

Tara smiled at Jesse's mom, and they both got up and made their way down the aisle to him. Those dark eyes were burning with emotion as he handed Tara his badge. Tears pricked the backs of her eyes as she secured it above his heart.

"Congratulations," she said as he hugged her.

"Can't believe you did all this," he whispered. "Love you."

She nodded and withdrew to let his mom have a chance. And watching them say hello after so long apart finally made a few of her tears fall. Happy tears. So much happiness.

When it was all over, the chief asked the whole class to stand and said, "May I introduce to you our newest officers and the 2019 graduates of the Metropolitan Police Academy!"

The room erupted in applause and everyone was instantly on their feet.

When it was over, Tara couldn't get enough of watching all his friends and loved ones congratulate Jesse. And, wow, seeing him with Willa, there was no denying that they were family. Jesse deserved this—all these reminders of the ways he *belonged*.

He certainly belonged to her. Just like she did to him.

The whole group partied and honored Jesse with a dinner, and then she and Jesse spent some time with his family at their hotel—the Marriott, of course. Tara so enjoyed seeing Jesse with his family that she couldn't help but think the evening ended way too soon.

"I'm sorry we can't stay longer," Willa said as she and her mom walked them to the door.

Jesse hugged his sister. "You don't have a thing to apologize for. I know you need to get out to California to get ready for your big day." That was where her fiancé, Max, owned a resort where the wedding was taking place, and they all had 6 AM cross-country flights the next morning. "And we'll see you there real soon."

"I know. I'm really proud of you, Jesse." She dashed away a tear before it fell.

He leaned down to meet his sister's eyes. "I'm really proud of you, too, Willa. And I'm so glad I get to be a part of your new family."

"Aw, geez, is everyone gonna get all mushy?" Alex said, making them all laugh. He didn't share Willa and Jesse's dark eyes, so Tara guessed he took after his father that way.

Jesse ruffled his nephew's hair. "Take care of your mama, little man."

"I will, Uncle Jesse," Alex said, giving Jesse a quick hug that made Tara's heart squeeze. Between wanting to sit by his uncle at dinner and all the stories Alex had told Jesse about his new dog, Rocky, it was clear the boy was enamored with his uncle. And Tara so cherished that for Jesse. She really did.

"I'll see you real soon, Jesse," his mom said next. When she pulled back from embracing Jesse, she reached out for Tara. "You have a sweet girl here." The lady gave her the warmest smile, one that made her feel like she was a real part of the reunion happening here. "I can't wait to see both of you again in a few weeks."

After that, everyone hugged again, until it was clear that no one really wanted to part. But finally, Jesse and Tara left and went home to her apartment—their temporary digs while they searched for a place together.

When they walked through the door, Penny and Mailman danced around their feet. The 10-year-old pug/terrier mix and 8-year-old pitty had been Jesse's idea, but it wasn't like it took much convincing for Tara to agree.

"Hi, guys," she said, bending down. "Jesse's a real police officer now, so you better be good." Mailman swiped his huge pink tongue across her chin, making her laugh.

Jesse chuckled. "They're in charge around here and they know it."

That much was true, which was why all four of them now slept in her bed. But as far as Tara was concerned, you could never have too much love.

"I'll take them out while you get changed," she said.

Jesse hesitated, but then just nodded. "Okay."

Fifteen minutes later, she returned with two much calmer doggos, and she was telling them what a good boy and girl they were when she walked through their apartment door—to find Jesse still in his uniform.

And down on one knee in the middle of the living room.

Tara gasped. She dropped the dogs' leashes, who didn't seem to mind dragging them along as they trotted to the water dish. "Jesse," she said.

He held out a hand, beckoning her to him. As her heart thundered in her chest, Jesse took her hand in his. "Tara Hunter, I love you for the amazing woman you are, for the man you've helped me become, and for all that you've given me. I'm a better man with you, and it would be the greatest honor of my life if you would let me dedicate my life to loving you. Tara, would you please marry me?"

Jesse pulled a diamond ring out of his pocket. The princess cut was stunning, perfect, but it couldn't begin to compare with the soul-deep love shining from this man's eyes. This man whom she loved with her whole heart.

"Nothing would make me happier, Jesse. Yes, I'll marry you," she said.

His breath actually caught, and the sound of his surprise and awe reached right into her chest. He slid the ring onto her finger and rose, taking her in his arms. "Love you, baby. So much. Thank you for taking a chance on me."

"Oh, Jesse, I love you, too. Loving you was the easiest thing I've ever done."

He took her chin in his fingers and smiled. "Here's looking at you, kid."

Yeah, they were meant to be.

THE END

* * * *

Also from 1001 Dark Nights and Laura Kaye, discover Ride Dirty, Hard As Steel, Hard To Serve, and Eyes On You.

Sign up for the 1001 Dark Nights Newsletter
and be entered to win a Tiffany Lock necklace.

There's a contest every quarter!

Go to www.1001DarkNights.com to subsribe.

As a bonus, all subscribers can download
FIVE FREE exclusive books!

Discover the Kristen Proby Crossover Collection

Soaring with Fallon: A Big Sky Novel
By Kristen Proby

Fallon McCarthy has climbed the corporate ladder. She's had the office with the view, the staff, and the plaque on her door. The unexpected loss of her grandmother taught her that there's more to life than meetings and conference calls, so she quit, and is happy to be a nomad, checking off items on her bucket list as she takes jobs teaching yoga in each place she lands in. She's happy being free, and has no interest in being tied down.

When Noah King gets the call that an eagle has been injured, he's not expecting to find a beautiful stranger standing vigil when he arrives. Rehabilitating birds of prey is Noah's passion, it's what he lives for, and he doesn't have time for a nosy woman who's suddenly taken an interest in Spread Your Wings sanctuary.

But Fallon's gentle nature, and the way she makes him laugh, and *feel* again draws him in. When it comes time for Fallon to move on, will Noah's love be enough for her to stay, or will he have to find the strength to let her fly?

* * * *

Wicked Force: A Wicked Horse Vegas/Big Sky Novella
By Sawyer Bennett

From *New York Times* and *USA Today* bestselling author Sawyer Bennett...

Joslyn Meyers has taken the celebrity world by storm, drawing the attention of millions. But one fan's affections has gone too far, and she's running to the one place she hopes he'll never find her – back home to Cunningham Falls.

Kynan McGrath leads The Jameson Group, a world-class security organization, and he's ready to do what it takes to keep Joslyn safe, even if it means giving up his own life in return. The one thing he's not prepared to lose, though, is his heart.

* * * *

Crazy Imperfect Love: A Dirty Dicks/Big Sky Novella
By KL Grayson

From *USA Today* bestselling author KL Grayson…

Abigail Darwin needs one thing in life: consistency. Okay, make that two things: consistency and order. Tired of being shackled to her obsessive-compulsive mind, Abigail is determined to break free. Which is why she's shaking things up.

Fresh out of nursing school, she takes a traveling nurse position. A new job in a new city every few months? That's a sure-fire way to keep her from settling down and falling into old habits. First stop, Cunningham Falls, Montana.

The only problem? She didn't plan on falling in love with the quaint little town, and she sure as heck didn't plan on falling for its resident surgeon, Dr. Drake Merritt

Laid back, messy, and spontaneous, Drake is everything she's not. But he is completely smitten by the new, quirky nurse working on the med-surg floor of the hospital.

Abby puts up a good fight, but Drake is determined to break through her carefully erected walls to find out what makes her tick. And sigh and moan and smile and laugh. Because he really loves her laugh.

But falling in love isn't part of Abby's plan. Will Drake have what it takes to convince her that the best things in life come from doing what scares us the most?

* * * *

Worth Fighting For: A Warrior Fight Club/Big Sky Novella
By Laura Kaye

From *New York Times* and *USA Today* bestselling author Laura Kaye…

Getting in deep has never felt this good...
Commercial diver Tara Hunter nearly lost everything in an accident that saw her medically discharged from the navy. With the help of the

Warrior Fight Club, she's fought hard to overcome her fears and get back in the water where she's always felt most at home. At work, she's tough, serious, and doesn't tolerate distractions. Which is why finding her gorgeous one-night stand on her new dive team is such a problem.

Former navy deep-sea diver Jesse Anderson just can't seem to stop making mistakes—the latest being the hot-as-hell night he'd spent with his new partner. This job is his second chance, and Jesse knows he shouldn't mix business with pleasure. But spending every day with Tara's smart mouth and sexy curves makes her so damn hard to resist.

Joining Tara's wounded warrior MMA training program seems like the perfect way for Jesse to blow off steam—except now they're getting in deep and taking each other down day and night. And even though it breaks all the rules, their inescapable attraction might just be the only thing truly worth fighting for.

* * * *

Nothing Without You: A Forever Yours/Big Sky Novella
By Monica Murphy

From *New York Times* and *USA Today* bestselling author Monica Murphy…

Designing wedding cakes is Maisey Henderson's passion. She puts her heart and soul into every cake she makes, especially since she's such a believer in true love. But then Tucker McCloud rolls back into town, reminding her that love is a complete joke. The pro football player is the hottest thing to come out of Cunningham Falls—and the boy who broke Maisey's heart back in high school.

He claims he wants another chance. She says absolutely not. But Maisey's refusal is the ultimate challenge to Tucker. Life is a game, and Tucker's playing to win Maisey's heart—forever.

* * * *

All Stars Fall: A Seaside Pictures/Big Sky Novella
By Rachel Van Dyken

From *New York Times* and *USA Today* bestselling author Rachel Van

Dyken...

She *left*.
Two words I can't really get out of my head.
She left *us*.
Three more words that make it that much worse.
Three being another word I can't seem to wrap my mind around.
Three kids under the age of six, and she left because she missed it. Because her dream had never been to have a family, no her dream had been to marry a rockstar and live the high life.

Moving my recording studio to Seaside Oregon seems like the best idea in the world right now especially since Seaside Oregon has turned into the place for celebrities to stay and raise families in between touring and producing. It would be lucrative to make the move, but I'm doing it for my kids because they need normal, they deserve normal. And me? Well, I just need a break and help, that too. I need a sitter and fast. Someone who won't flip me off when I ask them to sign an Iron Clad NDA, someone who won't sell our pictures to the press, and most of all? Someone who looks absolutely nothing like my ex-wife.

He's tall.
That was my first instinct when I saw the notorious Trevor Wood, drummer for the rock band Adrenaline, in the local coffee shop. He ordered a tall black coffee which made me smirk, and five minutes later I somehow agreed to interview for a nanny position. I couldn't help it; the smaller one had gum stuck in her hair while the eldest was standing on his feet and asking where babies came from. He looked so pathetic, so damn sexy and pathetic that rather than be star-struck, I took pity. I knew though; I knew the minute I signed that NDA, the minute our fingers brushed and my body became insanely aware of how close he was—I was in dangerous territory, I just didn't know how dangerous until it was too late. Until I fell for the star and realized that no matter how high they are in the sky—they're still human and fall just as hard.

* * * *

Hold On: A Play On/Big Sky Novella
By Samantha Young

From *New York Times* and *USA Today* bestselling author Samantha Young…

Autumn O'Dea has always tried to see the best in people while her big brother, Killian, has always tried to protect her from the worst. While their lonely upbringing made Killian a cynic, it isn't in Autumn's nature to be anything but warm and open. However, after a series of relationship disasters and the unsettling realization that she's drifting aimlessly through life, Autumn wonders if she's left herself too vulnerable to the world. Deciding some distance from the security blanket of her brother and an unmotivated life in Glasgow is exactly what she needs to find herself, Autumn takes up her friend's offer to stay at a ski resort in the snowy hills of Montana. Some guy-free alone time on Whitetail Mountain sounds just the thing to get to know herself better.

However, she wasn't counting on colliding into sexy Grayson King on the slopes. Autumn has never met anyone like Gray. Confident, smart, with a wicked sense of humor, he makes the men she dated seem like boys. Her attraction to him immediately puts her on the defense because being open-hearted in the past has only gotten it broken. Yet it becomes increasingly difficult to resist a man who is not only determined to seduce her, but adamant about helping her find her purpose in life and embrace the person she is. Autumn knows she shouldn't fall for Gray. It can only end badly. After all their lives are divided by an ocean and their inevitable separation is just another heart break away…

Discover 1001 Dark Nights Collection Six

DRAGON CLAIMED by Donna Grant
A Dark Kings Novella

ASHES TO INK by Carrie Ann Ryan
A Montgomery Ink: Colorado Springs Novella

ENSNARED by Elisabeth Naughton
An Eternal Guardians Novella

EVERMORE by Corinne Michaels
A Salvation Series Novella

VENGEANCE by Rebecca Zanetti
A Dark Protectors/Rebels Novella

ELI'S TRIUMPH by Joanna Wylde
A Reapers MC Novella

CIPHER by Larissa Ione
A Demonica Underworld Novella

RESCUING MACIE by Susan Stoker
A Delta Force Heroes Novella

ENCHANTED by Lexi Blake
A Masters and Mercenaries Novella

TAKE THE BRIDE by Carly Phillips
A Knight Brothers Novella

INDULGE ME by J. Kenner
A Stark Ever After Novella

THE KING by Jennifer L. Armentrout
A Wicked Novella

About Laura Kaye

Laura is the New York Times and USA Today bestselling author of nearly forty books in contemporary and erotic romance and romantic suspense, including the Raven Riders, Blasphemy, and Hard Ink series. Growing up, Laura's large extended family believed in the supernatural, and family lore involving angels, ghosts, and evil-eye curses cemented in Laura a life-long fascination with storytelling and all things paranormal. Laura also writes historical fiction as the NYT bestselling author Laura Kamoie. She lives in Maryland with her husband and two daughters, and appreciates her view of the Chesapeake Bay every day.

Learn more at www.LauraKayeAuthor.com

Join Laura's Newsletter for Exclusives & Giveaways!

Discover More Laura Kaye

Ride Dirty: A Raven Riders Novella

Caine McKannon is all about rules. As the Raven Riders' Sergeant-at-Arms, he prizes loyalty to his brothers and protection of his club. As a man, he takes pleasure wherever he can get it but allows no one close—because distance is the only way to ensure people can't hurt you. And he's had enough pain for a lifetime.

But then he rescues a beautiful woman from an attack.

Kids and school are kindergarten teacher Emma Kerry's whole life, so she's stunned to realize she has an enemy—and even more surprised to find a protector in the intimidating man who saved her. Tall, dark, and tattooed, Caine is unlike any man Emma's ever known, and she's as uncertain of him as she is attracted. As the danger escalates, Caine is in her house more and more – until one night of passion lands him in her bed.

But breaking the rules comes at a price, forcing Caine to fight dirty to earn a chance at love.

* * * *

Eyes On You: A Blasphemy Novella

She wants to explore her true desires, and he wants to watch…

When a sexy stranger asks Wolf Henrikson to rescue her from a bad date, he never expected to want the woman for himself. But their playful conversation turns into a scorching one-night stand that reveals the shy beauty gets off on the idea of being seen, even if she's a little scared of it, too. And Wolf loves to watch.

In the wake of discovering her fiancé's infidelity, florist Olivia Foster never expected to find someone who not only understood her wildest, darkest fantasies, but would bring them to life. As Wolf introduces her to his world at the play club, Blasphemy, Liv finds herself tempted to explore submission and exhibitionism with the hard-bodied Dom even as she's scared to trust again.

But Wolf is a master of getting what he wants—and he's got his eyes set on her…

* * * *

Hard As Steel: A Hard Ink/Raven Riders Crossover

After identifying her employer's dangerous enemies, Jessica Jakes takes refuge at the compound of the Raven Riders Motorcycle Club. Fellow Hard Ink tattooist and Raven leader Ike Young promises to keep Jess safe for as long as it takes, which would be perfect if his close, personal, round-the-clock protection didn't make it so hard to hide just how much she wants him--and always has.

Ike Young loved and lost a woman in trouble once before. The last thing he needs is alone time with the sexiest and feistiest woman he's ever known, one he's purposely kept at a distance for years. Now, Ike's not sure he can keep his hands or his heart to himself--or that he even wants to anymore. And that means he has to do whatever it takes to hold on to Jess forever.

* * * *

Hard To Serve: A Hard Ink Novella

To protect and serve is all Detective Kyler Vance ever wanted to do, so when Internal Affairs investigates him as part of the new police commissioner's bid to oust corruption, everything is on the line. Which makes meeting a smart, gorgeous submissive at an exclusive play club the perfect distraction…

The director of the city's hottest art gallery, Mia Breslin's career is golden. Now if only she could find a man to dominate her nights and set her body—and her heart—on fire. When a scorching scene with a hard-bodied, brooding Dom at Blasphemy promises just that, Mia is lured to serve Kyler again and again.

Then, as their relationship burns hotter, Kyler learns that he's been dominating the daughter of the hard-ass boss who has it in for him. Now Kyler must choose between life-long duty and forbidden desire before Mia finds another who's not so hard to serve.

Fighting for Everything
Warrior Fight Club
By Laura Kaye

This fight club has one rule: You might be a veteran...

Loving her is the biggest fight of his life...

Home from the Marines, Noah Cortez has a secret he doesn't want his oldest friend, Kristina Moore, to know. It kills him to push her away, especially when he's noticing just how sexy and confident she's become in his absence. But, angry and full of fight, he's not the same man anymore either. Which is why Warrior Fight Club sounds so good.

Kristina loves teaching, but she wants more out of life. She wants Noah—the boy she's crushed on and waited for. Except Noah is all man now—in ways both oh so good and troubling, too. Still, she wants who he's become—every war-hardened inch. And when they finally stop fighting their attraction, it's everything Kristina never dared hope for.

But Noah is secretly spiraling, and when he lashes out, it threatens what he and Kristina have found. The brotherhood of the fight club helps him confront his demons, but only Noah can convince the woman he loves that he's finally ready to fight for everything.

* * * *

"I'm no good right now, Kristina," Noah said in a low voice.

She shook her head. "That's not true. You've been through something horrible. And you're still recovering. Still hurting. That's all understandable—"

"I am fucked in the head. You saw it yourself. Twice," he said, his voice suddenly loud, bitter. Under her hands, his muscles tensed.

"You are not fucked in the head," she said, anger and determination gathering deep in her belly. Not anger at Noah, but irrational anger for him. She hated that things had happened to him that left him feeling this way. So out of control, so sad, so unlike himself. "Sure, you have things you're dealing with. And you *will* get a handle on them—"

"No," he said, shaking her off and pacing in the narrow space behind the door. "You don't understand. I'm…" Noah's hands squeezed into fists at his sides. "…so goddamned angry. All the time. It feels like I could tear the world to pieces. And I want to." He whirled on her. "Because the perfection of everything around me makes me feel so much more wrecked inside that I can barely breathe."

Oh, God.

Tears pricked at the backs of her eyes, but she wouldn't let them fall. She wouldn't let *herself* fall apart. Not now. Not in front of him. Not when Noah needed to lean on her so damn badly. "The world around you is not perfect, Noah. It's an illusion. And you are not wrecked—"

"I am." He got right up in her face.

Kristina held her ground. "You're not—"

"I am!"

"Noah—"

He grabbed her by the arms, not so much that it hurt, but with enough force that it surprised her. "Here's your proof. You're my best friend in the world, and I want to fuck you, Kristina. I want to bury myself in you and stay there forever. Just lose myself in you until I don't know who I am anymore. I've been fantasizing about it, dreaming about it, imagining it. Having you is all I can fucking think about. Do you understand what I'm saying?"

Noah's words unleashed a flash fire in Kristina's blood. Her heart tripped into a sprint. Her breathing shallowed out. Heat roared across her skin. One heartbeat. Two. And Kristina knew what she had to do.

On behalf of 1001 Dark Nights,

Liz Berry and M.J. Rose would like to thank ~

Steve Berry
Doug Scofield
Kim Guidroz
Jillian Stein
Social Butterfly PR
Dan Slater
Asha Hossain
Chris Graham
Fedora Chen
Kasi Alexander
Jessica Johns
Dylan Stockton
Richard Blake
and Simon Lipskar